Citizen Insane

A Barbara Marr Murder Mystery

Karen Cantwell

Citizen Insane

Cover art by Katerina Vamvasaki

Other books in the Barbara Marr Murder Mystery Series:

Take the Monkeys and Run (#1)
Citizen Insane (#2)
Silenced by the Yams (#3 - release date, December, 2011)

Acknowledgments

Thank you (a million times) to the many people who assisted me in bringing this novel to readers: Patrick Cantwell, Misha Crews, LC Evans, Moe and Linda Fraunfelder, Nancy Fulda, LB Gschwandtner, Michelle Hill, Linda Cupp Mihay, Colleen Tompkins, Maria Schneider, and Barbara Silkstone. I couldn't a done it withoutcha.

I dedicate this novel to my wonderful children.

Chapter One

There was a time when my life wasn't that exciting. I'm a soccer mom living in the suburbs. The only thrills in my day should be the frantic road races between ballet lessons and the much-too-closely-scheduled orthodontist appointment on the other side of the universe. If you think a stunt driver knows how to maneuver a vehicle, wait until you see me behind the wheel careening through yellow lights with a hundred-dollar dental visit at stake.

So, when I ran a woman down with my mini-van in the middle of the night, only to find out that someone else had tried to kill her with a 45 caliber semi-automatic pistol, I assumed things couldn't get any more dramatic. I assumed wrong. Just twenty-four hours later I found myself in the stairwell of an abandoned building, with a gun in my hand and a female hostage telling me to "do what Keanu would do." I've never met another mother with days like these.

My name is Barbara Marr and I find dead people.

Or, almost dead people.

But I'm getting ahead of myself. The story really started with my need for a foot rub.

On a sunny and cool Monday morning I sipped on coffee while suffering a broken heart and a pair of achy arches. Don't ask me why, but when I get upset, my feet start to hurt. When this happens, I generally turn to my husband Howard for a delicious foot rub. The sensation when he works his fingers around my toes, over the ball, and under my arch is nearly orgasmic. Howard was the reason for my despair, however, so instead, I scheduled a pedicure. Not just any pedicure – a Sweet Tangerine Spice Ultra-Ultimate Pedicure at La Voila Day Spa. It wouldn't end with a passionate tumble between the sheets like Howard's foot rubs did, but at least I'd get a good exfoliation.

The reason for my sorry state? Infidelity. I can't cook, sew, knit, crochet or hook rugs and I hate scrapbooking, but I love my three beautiful girls more than anything in life, and do a darn good job on the mothering front, even if I order in our Thanksgiving meals pre-cooked. I have a movie review website called ChickAtTheFlix.com that gets a couple hits a day (okay, maybe a week). And I am married to a man who I once believed to be faithful. However, after spying him through the window at Fiorenza's, sharing wine and fettucini with a well-endowed blond floozy, I was starting to have my doubts.

I suppose I brought it on myself. See, a few months ago, Howard revealed a twenty-five year long secret – he'd been raised Sammy Donato, the son of Mario Donato, who got whacked by one Tito Buttaro. And he wasn't an engineer working for a local government contractor, he was an FBI agent bent on finding his father's killer. Really. You can't make this stuff up.

Anyway, after that little discovery, I still loved him, but did I really know him? So I kicked him out and told him to date me and win back my affections. "Let's start over," I said.

Well, it seemed like a good idea at the time. Only, the dates were far and few between. His FBI job kept him too busy or out of town, often for weeks at a time. Some days I could barely remember what he looked like and would have to watch *Ocean's Eleven* just to feel close to him. That's because he bears a striking resemblance to George Clooney. I know – lucky me. Or not so lucky, evidently. Was it possible some other woman had snatched up my handsome husband while I was playing silly games? I wallowed in despair, wondering if I had lost him forever.

I was depressed and really needed that pedicure.

I looked at my watch and realized that spa time was right around the corner. My two cats, Indiana Jones and Mildred Pierce, were pacing and meowing, so I emptied a cup of food into each cat food bowl then slipped on my shoes. I was ready to step outside and check the weather when the phone rang. It was my neighbor, Roz Walker. I picked up the receiver.

"Hey," I said. "You ready for the foot massage of your life?"

"I'm ready, but while it's on my mind, do you have plans for tonight?" she asked.

"Other than rip Howard's Mr. McNuggets from his cheating body and throw them to a pack of hungry wild boar? No."

"Herd."

"Heard what?"

"No. It's a herd. A herd of wild boar."

"You know how to take the fun out of everything don't you?"

"Why don't you leave Howard's manliness intact, and come with me to the PTA meeting instead?"

I moaned loud enough for Bangladesh to hear. I hated PTA meetings. Not my gig. Roz was PTA president and my best friend and we'd stayed best friends because she had never asked me to attend.

"PLEASE!" she begged. "I promise, I'll never ask again, but I really need you there tonight. I need a friendly face in the crowd."

"Crowd? Isn't it only like, six people?"

"Eight, sometimes nine."

"Let's talk about it at the spa."

"No, I want to enjoy myself there and this just gets me too upset."

"What's the deal?"

"Yearbook scandal."

I laughed. "Yearbook scandal? What does that mean?"

"You're stalling. Will you please come?"

"Fine." I sighed. "I'll do it."

"Thank you! You're wonderful. And trust me, you won't be disappointed. More than tempers are going to fly at this meeting. Are you ready to leave? You're driving, right?"

"Yup. I'm just going to step outside to see if I need a jacket."

"I'll be right over."

I put the phone back into the cradle and opened the door that led to the breezeway connecting our house to the garage. My mother's intuition, and the fact that I could hear someone moaning, told me there was a problem in my yard. I quickly circled toward the front of my house, afraid Roz had been hurt.

I rounded the corner. "Roz?" I yelled.

No Roz. Just a strange lady whimpering and walking in circles on my front lawn. The operative word here is "strange." Unfortunately, this woman was not a stranger. I knew her – Bunny Bergen. She lived one street over and her kids went to the same school as mine. Towering close to six feet tall, she had a Cindy Crawford body and talked all breathy as if she were trying to be sexy, but really it just sounded like she was always on the verge of an asthma attack. Then there was the way she looked at me, unblinking and intense like a crocodile on crack. I had always considered Bunny Bergen an odd duck, and that was before I found her turning circles in front of my house like Mel Gibson after the bars closed.

Why? I thought. Why me? Didn't I have enough problems?

I watched her for another minute, trying to decide what her deal was. Maybe Bunny had rabies. She wasn't foaming at the mouth, but everything else sort of pointed to the possibility. I considered calling animal control. Maybe they'd shoot her with a tranquilizing dart and put us both out of her misery.

"Bunny?" I was careful to take slow steps. She was still circling neurotically and her mumblings became more audible as I approached.

"Poor Bunny, poor Bunny, poor Bunny," she wheezed.

That's when I spotted Roz in her signature floral print dress and tan loafers. She swatted at a gnat that buzzed her blonde, Dorothy Hamill bob then moved tentatively toward me. We exchanged silent what's-her-problem shrugs. Meanwhile, the demented woman seemed completely unaware that we were there. She kept turning and muttering. "Poor Bunny, poor Bunny, poor Bunny." Every second rotation or so she would stop, look up at the sky for a beat, then repeat the drill.

Roz and I traded helpless glances. What exactly was the protocol for dealing with crazy Bunnies? Call the police? St. Elizabeth's? Dr. Phil?

"What should we do?" whispered Roz.

I shrugged. "Nothing, I guess. We need to get going or we'll miss our appointment."

"We can't leave her here like this!"

"Why not? She'll find her way home. Eventually."

She narrowed her eyes. "Barb . . ."

I looked at my watch. Ten after eleven. Our pedicure appointments were scheduled for noon. Damn! We weren't rich, spoiled mothers who scheduled weekly manicures, pedicures, and chin-hair waxes. This was a special occasion, thanks to my three beautiful daughters who had each given me a gift certificate for Christmas. I had been saving them, and now – deep in the throes of marital misery – the time was right. No trippy twinkie was going to mess with my Sweet Tangerine Spice Ultra-Ultimate Pedicure at La Voila Day Spa. This Bunny was goin' down.

"Hey! Bunny!" I shouted.

She stopped turning, but her gaze was still fixed on the ground.

"Barb!" Roz whispered. "Be careful. She might be in shock."

I waved a dismissive hand. I knew what I was doing. Maybe.

Moving closer, I shouted again.

"Bunny!"

She looked at me and the tiny hairs on my neck sprung upright. It was the creepiest stare I'd ever seen. The proverbial lights were on but no one was in the *casa*. If I didn't know better, I would have thought we were in a low-budget zombie movie.

Now, I'm a true believer that life imitates art, and I love the art of film. That's why, when in doubt, I imitate the movies. This particular situation called for a little maneuver from one of my all time favorites, *Moonstruck*. Grabbing Bunny's face with both hands, I looked straight into her eerie, zombie eyes, and pulled out an impressive Cher impression. "Snapoutuvit!" I yelled.

Bingo! Like magic, Bunny's face changed and I knew she finally recognized me. Always trust a good screenwriter to get you out of a sticky situation.

"Barb?" she asked.

"Yeah, it's Barb. Listen, Bunny, you need to go home. We've got an appointment for pedicures."

"Barb!" Roz's forehead was all scrunched-up and screaming disapproval. She moved in to take control.

"Bunny," she said in a soothing, motherly voice, "What happened?"

Ah geez. She'd gone and done it. Not only was I feeling guiltier than the dog that ate the birthday cake, but I was fairly sure the very saintly and patient Roz was going to make us late for our Sweet Tangerine Spice Ultra-Ultimate Pedicures. Yes, she was probably doing the right thing, and yes, she was a wonderful person for it, but truth be told, I just didn't care for Bunny Bergen.

First, there was her name. Come on. Bunny? What grown woman allows herself to be called Bunny? Supposedly, her real name was Bertha. Okay, not so good, but really – isn't Bert or Bertie better than Bunny? Eesh.

Then there was her obsequious and always-happy attitude, not to mention the fact that she had the body of a super-model. No single person should be that happy and stunning to boot, especially after giving birth twice. It threw off the balance of nature.

Finally, there was the issue of her questionable source of income. She was a Marrier – she married then made her money from the subsequent divorces. No one knew for sure, but it had been estimated that she had four divorces under her diamond-studded Gucci belt. Supposedly she had more lawyers than Joan Rivers had plastic surgeons.

So, yes, I had trouble working up enough sympathy to justify missing my special treat-of-the-year. It was, after all, a Sweet Tangerine Spice Ultra-Ultimate Pedicure. Ultra-Ultimate.

Problem was, Roz was making me look bad. Rubbing Bunny on the back, talking in soothing tones. Being nice. I finally decided I had no alternative other than to join Roz and see the Bunny rescue to the end.

"Bunny?" Roz was asking, "Do you know where you are?"

Bunny did a visual scan of the area, then nodded and sniffed a little. "This is Barb's house, right?"

"Yeah, it's my house. That's good, we're making progress," I said, still having trouble feeling the moment. "What's your problem?"

Roz shot me a glare fit to kill.

I reworded the question. "I mean, are you okay?"

"I . . . hit a bunny," she whispered after a moment of silence, as if she was sharing a terrible secret.

"A rabbit?" Roz whispered back. "You hit a rabbit?"

Bunny nodded and tears started rolling down her cheeks.

I'm a sucker for tears, and I had to admit, this poor woman was starting to get to me. "How?" I asked.

"With my car."

I looked around. You couldn't miss it brand spanking new, gold Jaguar convertible. No Jag in my driveway or on the street.

"Where?" I asked.

The Bunn-ster went all glassy on us again. I threw my arms in the air, exasperated. Roz took over. She moved closer and attempted to put an arm around Bunny's shoulders, which wasn't easy, since Bunny was about seven inches taller than her. The whole thing was just too awkward, so she eventually settled for patting Bunny lightly on the lower back.

"Bunny?" Roz's tone was far calmer and more comforting than mine. "Bunny? Where did you hit the bunny?"

"I was driving home. I turned into my driveway then it was just there. Like out of nowhere. And there was nothing I could do. I hit the bunny."

Bunny hit a bunny. See? This is what I mean. How can a person take such a scenario seriously? People with animal names risk this ridiculous sort of redundancy, that's all I'm saying.

"How did you end up here?" Roz asked.

"I walked through the woods," she continued. "I needed Howard. Is he here?"

Howard? My blood started to boil. Why did she want my husband? Wasn't 911 good enough for her?

First that blond bimbo in the restaurant last night, now Bunny Bergen. It seemed that Howard had become The Roaming Romancer of Rustic Woods, Virginia. I had lost him to skanky tramps on the prowl for handsome, lonely husbands.

While deciding whether to answer Bunny's question or land a hard fist onto her pretty, plump, collagen-injected kisser, a cell phone started to ring. It was coming from Roz's sweater.

"Get that, will you?" She was still patting Bunny's back.

I slipped the phone out of her pocket and took a quick peek at the caller ID. It was our friend Peggy who was joining us for pedicure day.

"Hey," I answered, hand on my hip and grumpy frown on my face.

"Ciao, baby," she answered back in her usual bouncy tone. Peggy is a woman who embraces people, ideas and cultures with a passion. She converted to Judaism before marrying Simon Rubenstein, then after honeymooning across Italy, my red-headed, fair skinned, Irish-descended friend took to the Italian culture as if she'd been born into it. She often forgets that her maiden name was O'Malley, not Minnelli. Like most Italians, Peggy has a vivacious joy for life.

"I'm just leaving my house," she continued, "You want I should drive around and pick up you two lovely Signoras?"

"Come on over, but we've encountered a bit of a . . . problem," I said.

"Problem? Please tell me you haven't found more monkeys!" She was laughing.

"Not monkeys. Bunnies."

Just then Bunny started wailing again.

"What was that?" Peggy asked.

I circled around and lowered my voice. "Just get over here. You can see for yourself."

"Be there in a flash."

Peggy lived two streets over on Dogwood Blossom Court. She would probably be in my driveway before I could dial the zoo to tell them I'd found their lost cuckoo bird.

Meanwhile, Roz, the ever wonderful and patient mother, patted and cooed and eventually soothed the unstable Bunny. I looked at my watch. Twenty after eleven. Forty minutes until our appointments. We still had time to wrap up this fruit cake, whip her home in Peggy's van, tear off to La Voila Day Spa, and plant our tooshies into those cozy massage chairs with just seconds to spare. Sweet Tangerine Spice Ultra-Ultimate Pedicures could still be ours. There is a God.

Peggy's green Town and Country van turned into the driveway.

"Okay," I said, turning back to Roz and Bunny. "Here's the plan. Bunny, you need rest. You come with Roz, okay? We're going to take you home. Is that okay with you?"

She nodded. It was a slow, sort of half-nod, but I was taking it.

"Roz, stay here with Bunny for just a minute, I'm going to convince Peggy to help us take Bunny back to her house."

I popped over to Peggy's van. She had rolled her window down. I didn't waste any time. "Here's the scoop: Bunny Bergen ran over a rabbit with her Jag and snapped. Meltdown. She came looking for Howard. I'd kill her, but we don't have time – I want my pedicure. If we can take her back to her house in your van, we can still make it to La Voila in time – you game?"

Peggy didn't answer, just stared at Bunny. Admittedly, it was a lot to throw at a person all at once.

"Peggy – they're Ultra-Ultimate Pedicures. Ultra. Ultra. They'll soak our feet in that warm wax, then rub them and scrub them until we're almost asleep in those womb-like chairs. Remember what it was like, before kids? When we had money to throw away on luxuries? We can't miss this. I'm all for leaving her here, but Roz has this whole Mother Teresa thing going on . . ."

"Yeah, get her in the van. Do you have the gift certificates?"

"I'll get them. You help Roz."

Peggy helped Roz guide Bunny into the back seat while I ran into the house and grabbed my purse and the ever precious gift certificates. I locked up the house lickety-split.

By the time I got back Peggy was in the driver's seat buckling up and Roz and Bunny were seated awkwardly on the middle bench. I hopped into the front passenger seat.

Bunny's house was less than a minute away. With just some extra gas to the engine, we could be there in no time, then on our way to Heaven.

"Come on Peggy," I said. "I feel the need! The need for speed!"

Peggy put her gear shift into reverse and we were on our way.

Roz rolled her eyes. "You and your *Shot Gun* quotes. Do you think we should be leaving her alone?"

"First off, it's *Top Gun*," I corrected her. "Don't you EVER watch movies?" It was my turn to roll some eyes. "Secondly, she's looking much better to me. We'll sit her down with a cup of tea and she'll be fine." I looked at Bunny who was rubbing her head. "Bunny, you okay?"

Her response, although slower than I would have liked, was positive.

"Yeah. I'm . . . I'm okay. I'm . . . well . . . I'm, you know . . . embarrassed. I just don't understand."

"Don't understand what?"

"Why I'm . . . in this van."

"Do you remember walking through the woods?"

She shook her head.

"Do you remember a rabbit?"

She shook her head again.

"Do you remember asking about Howard?"

Her face went red. She shook her head yet again. "Why would I . . . ask about Howard? He's your husband."

"Yeah, my thoughts exactly." Suppressing an urge to reach back and strangle her skinny little neck, I started to query her further, but was interrupted by Peggy.

"Uh oh," she said. "This can't be good."

Scooting back around, I agreed. Either an accident had occurred or else someone's house was on fire. Red lights flashed on fire trucks – I counted two of them. There was also a fire rescue vehicle and an ambulance. As we got closer, I realized they were parked right in front of Bunny's house. Two black sedans with more antennae than a radio station and a Fairfax County police car topped off the circus.

All of this for a dead rabbit?

I put the gift certificates to my mouth and kissed those Sweet Tangerine Spice Pedicures goodbye.

Chapter 2

"I thought I heard sirens a few minutes ago," Roz said.

"Who could hear anything with Bunny wailing like a cat in heat?" As soon as the words were out of my mouth, I regretted them. The comment was unkind. Roz shot me a look to shame, and rightly so. I whispered under my breath. "Sorry."

Peggy slowed to a near crawl and whistled. "Hey girls, look at the sexy cop in the sunglasses. If I weren't married . . ."

Dressed in a black suit, hands in his pockets, revealing a gun in a chest holster, and moving toward an unmarked car, was a man I had known for over twenty years. I slapped Peggy hard.

"That's not a sexy cop. That's my husband."

"That's Howard?" She squinted for a better look. "He cleans up nice. You know, it's really true – he does look like George Clooney."

Roz piped up from the back. "Why is Howard here?"

"I don't know, but I'm going to find out." Full of fury, I bounded out of the van and slammed the passenger-side door a little too hard behind me. "Sorry, Peggy!" I yelled as I stomped forward, eyes focused on Howard. He stood at one of the two unmarked cars, talking to a uniformed policeman.

Green Ashe Place was a much longer street than my own White Willow Circle. Bunny's monstrosity of a house was third from the left. She had one of the largest properties in the neighborhood: over an acre of land graced by an enormous brick front colonial house. Two tall white pillars added a hint of dignified Southern charm to the enviable homestead that sat back nearly two hundred feet from the street. A long macadam driveway made a bee-line to her three-car garage.

The flashing, rumbling emergency vehicles lined both sides of the street, while the police cruiser blocked access to Bunny's house. Howard's car was parked behind a fire engine on the right hand side of the road, not far from where we had stopped.

The problem was, Peggy was right. Howard always looked incredibly sexy when he wore a suit, sunglasses and a gun. And the FBI badge on his hip really got my juices flowing. The whole hot-guy crime fighter look was new and always robbed me of a breath or two. By the time I reached his side, the wind had practically gone out of my angry sails.

"Barb! What are you doing here?"

"I live in this neighborhood remember? What are YOU doing here?"

"Official business." He looked at the van. "Is that Peggy?"

"Yeah. And Roz. And . . . a friend." I coughed. "Of sorts."

"Get back in the van and have Peggy take you home. I'll come over and see you when I'm done here."

He went in for a kiss. I stopped him at the pass.

"Uh, we can't go. We have a crazy lady in the car. She showed up on my doorstep all loopy and asking for . . . who was she asking for again?" I tapped my forehead in mock forgetfulness. "Think, think, who was she asking for?" I snapped my fingers. "Oh! That's right. She was looking for YOU! Why would she be looking for you, Howard?"

"Bunny Bergen? Is Bunny Bergen in that van?" At the mention of Bunny's name, every suited and uniformed man within hearing distance looked in our direction.

I squinted suspiciously. "What's going on here?"

Howard grabbed my elbow and moved back while motioning to a blue-jacketed EMT standing beside the ambulance. "Can I get your help over here? Bring a blanket." He turned to face me. "Barb, tell me what happened."

"How's the fettucini at Fiorenza's?"

His body stiffened. He blinked three times then looked away.

"I went out for dessert with Roz and Peggy last night," I continued. "You know that yummy lava cake at Scottie's Pub?"

He turned back to me, his jaw set hard, but his dark eyes soft, revealing a whisper of emotion. Was it guilt? "Barb, let me—"

"Parking was hard to find though, so we left the car over by Fiorenza's."

"I can explain."

"Which of course, meant we had to walk past Fiorenza's to get to Scottie's."

"Listen to me—"

"I always look into Fiorenza's when I walk by, because, as you know, a person is likely to see a familiar face in there. It's such a popular restaurant and all."

"Do you want to hear what I have to say?"

"No, Romeo, I don't. Keep your dalliances to yourself, just don't go on pretending that this marriage means anything to you."

Howard's face reddened like coals when they're stoked. His fists tightened. Not that I thought he'd hit me – he wasn't the wife-hitting sort. But I'd made him mad. Plenty mad. He was silent for a few seconds (it seemed like years) while he stared at me with those intense, deep brown eyes. I stood my ground, though. I was the woman wronged, after all.

Finally, he spoke. Slow and deliberate like Christopher Walken on sedatives. "I'm on duty and have a job to do. We'll talk about this later. Now what happened with Bunny Bergen?"

"I found her in our front yard mumbling and acting like Rainman when he missed Jeopardy. Said she ran over a rabbit in her driveway, so she came over to our house looking for you. Do I need to ask why she was looking for you? Casanova?"

"Is she in the backseat?"

"Yeah, with Roz."

"Is she calm?"

"Now she is. I guess. You didn't answer my question."

Howard finally gave directions to the EMT who stared awkwardly at the sky during our little lovers spat. "She's in the backseat. See if she needs care."

Then he guided me toward the passenger side of the van. He brought his face close to mine and spoke in hushed tones. "Listen to me. Go back to the house and stay there – all three of you. I'll have to send Agent Bell over to take statements." He pointed to a tall, suited man who also wore an FBI badge and said with a half-hearted smile, "Don't worry, he's a good guy."

I wasn't warming to Howard's stab at humor but his cologne was starting to bake my cookies. Fighting the urge to jump him and give everyone a show, I played coy. "Can't wait."

He stopped me as I headed back toward the van. "Barb?"

"What?"

"I'll come by tonight and explain."

"Fine. But I promised Roz I'd go to the PTA meeting, so it will have to be after."

"You hate PTA meetings."

"I do. She needs me there. Some problem with the yearbook."

"The yearbook at Tulip Tree Elementary? What's the problem? You're not involved are you?" His concern seemed oddly out of place. He was probably trying to feign interest in my life to throw me off the scent of his philandering.

"Slow down law man – I have no idea what the problem is. It's a grade school yearbook for crying out loud. The company probably made the margins too wide. But I'll be sure to alert you and your Bureau buddies if it looks like any federal laws were broken."

He relaxed and came in again for a smooch, but I still wasn't obliging. I needed to hear his story first.

By the time I had plopped back into Peggy's van, Bunny was long gone.

Peggy was spewing questions before I had the door closed. "Holy canoli, girl! What's going on? Why are they here? What did Howard say?"

"I don't know, I don't know, and nothing. I take that back – he did say that we have to go back to my house until an agent comes and asks us questions."

Roz put her face between the two front seats. "Questions about what?"

"Bunny, I guess."

"Did you ask him about last night?"

I leaned my head back and closed my eyes. "I don't want to talk about it right now."

"Understood," Peggy said. She backed into a nearby driveway and spun around. "Well, this certainly did turn out to be an exciting day anyway, huh?" Leave it to Peggy to see the bright side of things.

My head throbbed mercilessly. "I need wine. A big, big glass of wine. Forget the glass. I need a vat of wine."

Roz, always the level-headed one, put her two cents in. "You need to eat something first."

My eyes were still closed, but I could feel us turning into my driveway.

"What the heck is that?" asked Peggy.

"What?" I opened my eyes.

A yellow, rusting Volkswagen van was parked in front of the garage. I'd never seen it before, but I knew the leather-coated man standing at my front door. Somehow, the man and the vehicle didn't match, but nothing about this day seemed normal.

"Barb . . ." Fear quivered in Roz's voice. "Is that who I think it is . . ."

Peggy didn't hide her panic. She slammed the breaks hard and tightened her grip on the wheel. "Maybe we should go back and get Howard for protection."

I slapped my forehead and fought the urge to scream to the heavens. First Bunny Bergen showed up in my front yard desperately seeking a sanity transplant, then I missed my Sweet Tangerine Spice Ultra-Ultimate Pedicure, and now a pug-faced Mafia thug had decided to pay me a little visit. Why?

Surely someone up there hated me.

Chapter 3

Roz had every reason to be afraid of the man, Frankie Romano. Not too long ago, he had sprained her wrist when he and his sidekick, Elvis Scarletti, kidnapped us by order of lady organized crime boss, Viviana Buttaro. Mafiosi in the suburbs of Virginia. Who knew? Very scary ordeal. I could write a book.

On the other hand, Frankie and Elvis eventually helped me assist the FBI in bringing down the chain-smoking, spikey-heeled Viviana and her cohort group of corrupt pharmaceutical executives, so I knew that Frankie wasn't really such a bad guy after all. In fact, I learned later that he had a serious aversion to killing, so we were never really in danger of being whacked. Regardless, Roz and Peggy still quaked in their seats.

Unbuckling the seatbelt, I tried to offer some consolation. "It's okay. He's harmless – I'll go talk to him. You stay here."

Frankie had watched us drive up. He stood, looking uneasy, with a lasagna pan in his hands. He had a face like a pug-dog, but dressed himself smartly in a black leather jacket and shiny shoes that surely boasted designer labels. "Mrs. Marr . . . nice to see you."

"Don't call me that, Frankie. We were tied up together, you threw up on my back, and we got shot at with an AK by a guy named No Toes – I think you can call me Barb."

He smiled. "How you doin' Barb?"

"I'm . . . good. I guess. Where's Elvis?"

"Went back to Philly. He never was a fan of dis place you know."

I nodded as if I really knew the guy well enough to understand that comment. "So, um . . . what brings you by?"

He cleared his throat. "I brought you dis. It's for you and your friends." He handed me the warm pan. The aroma of basil and cheese wafted upward and tickled my nosehairs. My stomach roared like a hungry lion.

"Is dat them in dat mini-van there?" He asked.

Looking at Peggy's van, I laughed. "That's them. They're still kind of afraid of you."

"Dat's why I'm here," Frankie said, putting his hands in his pockets. "I'm turnin' over a new leaf. Makin' amends. I got me a list – you know, like dat guy on the the TV show dats talkin' about karma all the time."

"So you brought us a lasagna to make amends?"

"No! Dat's baked ziti. It's my specialty. I got me a real job – I'm da chef over at dis place you mighta heard of. Fiorenza's."

"Really? We eat there all the time." So does my husband and his bimbo girlfriends, I thought.

"No kiddin'? Well next time you're there, ask for me – I'll make you a real special dish."

I felt a little uncomfortable at the thought of forging a friendship with Frankie the ex-mobster, even if he hadn't been the murdering kind.

"Oh!" Frankie's face lit up and he started to pull something out of his pants pocket. "I forgot I wanted to give you something else, here." The first time I met Frankie, he pulled a gun out of that pocket. Today he produced a chunk of business cards and handed me one. It read simply: Frankie Romano. Below his name was a phone number. "You call me should you have a need – anytime you need anything. Well, nothin' illegal as I'm turnin' over the new leaf and all. But, I would like if I could give one of these to each of them ladies there too. Especially the lady whose hand I mangled. I feel awful bad about dat."

Looking back at Roz and Peggy, I saw the terrified expressions on their faces had not weakened, despite our friendly exchange of food and business cards. "You know, I think it's best if we build them up to you gradually. Let me give them the cards after you leave, and I'll tell Roz – that's the lady whose wrist you sprained – I'll pass on your apologies to her. Maybe in a couple of weeks we'll stop by Fiorenza's and say 'Hi.' Or something."

Frankie's smile filled his face. "Yeah?"

"Yeah."

"And you call me anytime, you hear?"

"Absolutely."

The big lug moved in and hugged me so tight I thought I might drop the baked ziti on his designer shoes.

"Well, I'll go then. Need to get to work. Get ready for the dinner crowd."

I patted his back. "You do that."

Frankie practically skipped to his Volkswagen, grinning and waving at Peggy and Roz as he passed. Each gave a very hesitant and tentative wave back.

After he puttered away in his clunker, they left the safety of Peggy's van and followed me into my house.

"What was that?" asked Roz.

"Evidently he's traded in his shiny Lincoln Town Car and life of crime for an old Volkswagen and some good karma. He says he's sorry about your wrist. Now let's eat baked ziti! I'm starved."

We'd polished off the ziti and were sipping on glasses of Pinot Grigio by the time Agent Bell showed up to question us about Bunny Bergen and her apparent mental breakdown. We needled him for information, but he was a stone-faced, pinch-lipped bugger. No fun at all, and definitely not coughing up the goods, so when he thanked us for our time and I closed the door behind him, we were still left wondering "Why had Bunny snapped?"

Back at my kitchen table, Peggy and Roz were scratching at remnants of ziti. I looked at the clock above the sink. "Two-fifty five. Callie's bus will be here in five minutes."

Roz took another healthy swig from her glass. "That gives us thirty five minutes until the younger kids get home. I need this wine – it will calm me for the PTA meeting tonight." She looked at Peggy. "Barb is coming – please come too. I need reinforcements."

"Sorry. Can't. I've got book club at Cappucino Corner."

"How many book clubs do you belong to?" Roz asked.

She counted on her fingers. "Five. But they all have different themes. Tonight is Italian Heritage book club."

"Peggy," I said, "You do know that you're not Italian, right?"

Peggy leaned in, clearly pleased that I had brought up the subject. "Actually, I've been researching my family tree and interviewing relatives in Ireland. It turns out, that my great, great, great Aunt Fianna had a sister whose name no one can remember, but her daughter went off to Italy one summer and when she came back, she was pregnant. Well, actually, no one is sure if she was pregnant, because they're pretty much all dead now, but the story is that somehow all of the sudden, BOOM, she had a baby girl and it had dark hair and a big nose. Oh, and she had an Italian accent."

I shook my head. "The baby had an Italian accent?"

"No, the daughter."

Roz was confused too. "Whose daughter?"

"My great, great, great Aunt Fianna's sister's daughter."

"So, your great, great, great Aunt Fianna's niece?" asked Roz.

"I guess you could look at it that way."

Roz was getting into the tangled tale. "So according to people who are dead now, your great, great, great Aunt Fianna's niece went to Italy, came back with an accent, then had a baby girl with a big nose and dark hair?"

"Exactly."

"Peggy," I said, "that's got to be the strangest story you've ever told."

"Yes, but it shows a family connection to Italy. Where there's one connection, there could be more, that's all I'm saying."

Peggy took a sip of the Pinot while Roz and I stared at her, unable to make a reasonable response to her family connection conclusion.

"So I can't join you at the meeting," she said putting her glass down. "Why do you need reinforcements?"

Roz rubbed her eyes then ran a hand through her hair. "Big yearbook scandal."

"Scandal?" I asked. "You keep using that word. Just how scandalous can a yearbook be, really?"

"Oh, very scandalous. You don't know these parents. High strung. Uptight. Type-A. Oh, why me?" She plunked her head down on my table.

"Would you just tell us the sob story, already?"

Roz tilted her head so she could talk, but left it on the table. "Krystle Jennings was the yearbook committee chair."

"She moved, right?" Peggy asked.

"Disappeared is more like it. Do you have a tissue? I think I'm getting a cold."

"In the bathroom."

Roz continued to talk, just more loudly, from my bathroom in between blows of her nose. "One day she and her son were there, the next day they weren't."

"Where did they live?" I hollered.

She returned, her nose red and swollen, sat down and took another sip before answering. "A small house over on Pinoak Terrace."

"Did she sell it?" Peggy asked.

She shook her head. "Didn't own it. She rented. And I heard that she skipped out on three months rent." She took another swipe at her nose with the tissue.

"So where's the PTA scandal?"

"You know the candid pictures? Of the students at The Fall Fair, Science Night, in their classrooms, in the hallways? The kids get the yearbook and start flipping through looking for pictures of themselves having fun with their friends?"

"Yeah. . . ." I wasn't quite sure where this story was going.

"Not this year. We got the proofs back right after she skipped town. Every single picture in that book, other than class pictures, is of her son."

Peggy cringed. "Is he that kid with the big ears and . . . how do I put this delicately . . . unruly teeth?"

"That would be him."

"Every single picture?"

"Every picture."

"Can't you send in new pictures?"

"Too late. She made the final deadline approvals all by herself."

"Can't the yearbook company do something?"

"Nothing that will get us yearbooks before school is out."

"Uh, oh."

"Yeah. Most of these moms join the committee specifically to squirm their way in with the yearbook chair and guarantee their kids pictures in prime spots. They are going to be so pissed. I'm not a violent woman, but I tell you this – if I EVER see Krystle Jennings again, I swear I'll hurt her. I'll hurt her very badly."

Our silent contemplation of Krystle Jennings' nefarious yearbook sabotage was interrupted by the familiar slamming and thumping that always accompanied my teenage Callie's after-school entrance. For a gracefully slim and generally quiet girl, she could rouse up a cacophony akin to an elephant stampede.

"Tadaima!"

A Junior at Forest Glen High School, Callie had taken to her beginning Japanese language class with unexpected enthusiasm. While I was pleasantly surprised at the amount of attention she paid to the subject, I did suspect it had more to do with the teacher, Mr. Obayashi, who was a very handsome and charming young man who barely looked twenty himself.

"What does that mean?" I yelled back.

She popped her pretty face into the kitchen doorway. She was a younger, feminine version of Howard to be sure. Hair the color of dark chocolate – thick and wavy. Perfect nose. Intense dark, almost black eyes and flawless skin, even at fifteen. I should have been so lucky at her age.

"It means, I'm home," Callie translated. "Oh, and Grandma's here."

"You said all of that with one word?"

"No. I mean, Grandma IS here. She drove up a second ago."

Peggy and Roz jumped up from the table and grabbed their purses.

"Gotta run," Roz said.

"Me too. Things to do," Peggy said with fear in her eyes.

I looked at my clock again. The elementary school bus wouldn't arrive for another half hour. "You guys have twenty minutes at least. You're leaving because of my mother, aren't you?"

They exchanged glances. Roz spoke. "She scares us. She's so . . . what's the word . . ."

"Tall," Peggy assisted Roz with their excuse.

"Yes," agreed Roz. "And . . ."

"Forceful." Peggy slipped her thin sweater on so fast that it bunched up and hung all lopsided.

"Forceful," nodded Roz. "That's a good word."

"Better than pushy and overbearing I guess." I shrugged.

"We'll just slip out your back door. Ciao!" Peggy was gone in a flash.

"See you at the bus stop." Roz zipped out behind her waving.

I gave her a dirty look. She slammed the sliding glass door just as my mother swished in the front.

"Hello? Anyone home?" She hollered out, knowing perfectly well that I was.

Before I could get my act together or hide, she was standing over me surveying the empty wine bottle.

"Drinking in the middle of the day?" She shook her head and clicked her tongue. "This isn't good. This isn't good at all."

My mother commands quite a presence. She towers over my five foot eight inch frame. She's a freakishly tall, big boned woman. Not fat, just big. Everything she does is big – she dresses big and lavish, she walks big, she talks big. As a young girl growing up, I felt dwarfed by the shadow of her character, only thankful that I didn't inherit her monstrously large physical frame. Right now, I felt about three years old.

I learned early in life that the best way to deal with my mother's comments was to ignore them.

"What brings you by, Mom?"

"Do I need a reason to visit my only daughter and grandchildren?"

"No, but you usually have one anyway."

"Nope. Nope. No reason." She sat down while giving the room a cursory visual inspection. "Not really."

"Not really?"

"No, but while I'm here, I might as well mention that I met a very nice, handsome, respectable and SINGLE man the other day. How about I set you two up?"

"I'm married!"

"You wouldn't know it. When was the last time Howard was here, anyway?"

Unfortunately, I didn't answer quickly because I really couldn't remember. He had been called out of town on lengthy assignments twice since Christmas. And more recently he'd been working some long hours, or so he said. Of course, I now knew he was probably working long hours romancing bodacious bimbos. I wasn't going to tell my mother that, however. So I punted. "I just saw him a couple of minutes ago, as a matter of fact."

She didn't seem convinced. "Howard should take a lesson from the way your father lived his life. Your father never would have left his family like this. He was a good, honest and dedicated family man, rest his dear soul."

My sweet father, who was a small man compared to most, died in his sleep three years ago, supposedly of sleep apnea. I always suspected that maybe my mother accidentally rolled on top of him in the middle of the night, smothering the life out of him.

"Mom, Howard didn't leave me. This is all my doing. I told him to live at the condo so we could explore our relationship through dating again. I thought we'd learn to appreciate each other again and make our marriage stronger."

"Dear, excuse me for being blunt, but that's the dumbest idea you've ever had."

Sadly, she was right, but I would never admit that fact to her. I rubbed my weary eyes. "Whatever, Mom."

"What do you plan to do about it?"

"I don't know, but I don't have time to talk about it now, I have to walk up to the bus stop. Amber and Bethany's bus will be here any minute."

"Do you mind if I use your phone?"

"Go ahead."

The sun had warmed the air nicely over the day. I stood on the front walk, closed my eyes, and took some deep cleansing breaths, concentrating on the joys of Spring rather than the woes of Barbara Marr.

My silent reverie was shattered by a voice right next to my ear.

"It looks like you have company."

I jumped and screamed, my heart racing a million miles a minute. The voice came from my nosy "friend" Waldo. He was easily three inches shorter than me, with fuzzy, dark hair that hovered over his eyes like a flying saucer, a waxy complexion that made him look sickly, and a wardrobe that screamed for a fashion consultant. Even though he was new to the neighborhood, he'd already succeeded in meeting just about every married woman within a two-mile radius and offering himself as "someone to listen" since he was a psychotherapist by trade.

"Waldo! Don't scare me like that."

"I'm so sorry. I would never mean to scare you." He pointed at the red GTO convertible pulling in behind my mother's Mini Cooper. I knew that GTO well. And its driver, my friend and Howard's roommate, Colt Baron. Colt is just plain yummy. Blond, wispy hair and a smile that makes a woman's heart palpitate. Women fall for Colt everywhere he goes. He's also a private investigator who agreed to teach me how to shoot a hand gun. I assumed this was the reason for his visit.

"Hey, Curly!" Colt flashed his smile as he bounded up the walkway like a happy puppy. He and Waldo slipped me awkward I-don't-know-him glances, so I felt obligated to make introductions.

"Waldo, this is my friend Colt. Colt this is –"

"Oswald Fuchs," he interrupted, thrusting his hand toward Colt. "But you can call me Waldo. That way, when you're wondering where I am, you can just say, 'Where's Waldo?'" He laughed at his own joke. It was his standard line and, since I had already heard it at least ten times, it was really becoming a sore point with me. Mostly because I felt required to laugh at it every time even though what I really wanted to do was stick my finger in his eye like Moe giving it to Larry.

Colt took Waldo's hand, but I could see he wasn't impressed. "Nice to meet you." He dismissed Waldo quickly turning to me, "You got a minute?"

I nodded. "You can walk with me to the bus stop. Waldo, I have to go. Did you . . . want something?"

He just grinned and shook his head. "Nope."

"Okay, then." I started walking, hoping he'd get the message and skedaddle. "See ya later."

The message wasn't received. "I hear there was quite a commotion over at Bunny Bergen's house today," he said. "Do you know what happened there?"

I stiffened a little.

"Really?" I said. "A commotion? I don't know anything about that."

"You don't?" Waldo looked puzzled. "Maria Nichols told me that fire engines and police were swarming around her house. She said a medic pulled Bunny out of Peggy Rubenstein's van while you talked to someone who looked like George Clooney. Doesn't your husband look like George Clooney?"

Colt stifled a laugh.

"Listen, Waldo, I'm really not supposed to be talking about this. Best if you left it alone."

"I'm just so concerned about poor Bunny." He clicked his long, gross fingernails. "Hopefully the incident wasn't related to her obsession with Howard."

Chapter 4

Waldo slapped a hand over his mouth.

"What?" My right eye twitched once.

"I shouldn't have said that."

"But you did." Twitch.

"Pretend you didn't hear it."

"I can't."

He checked his watch. "I put a flan in the oven before taking my walk. Must take it out. Be good, stay healthy and nurture the spirit within you." Waldo touched my forehead lightly then turned and sprinted through the woods on the path that led back to his own house.

Colt watched him scurry away. "Never trust a man that makes flan."

"I need a vacation – from life." My cheek puckered, indicating the genesis of a cry. We trekked down my driveway toward the road.

"What was that all about?"

"Long story." I stopped. "Is Howard having an affair? Tell me the truth."

"Oh, geez."

"I saw him last night in a restaurant getting all cozy with a blonde."

"Shouldn't you be asking him this question? Remember that talk we had about putting me in the middle? I'm just the roommate."

We did make that agreement. It worked for more reasons than one. Like the fact that even after many, many years, Colt still carried a strongly lit torch for me. "You're right. I'm sorry."

Roz was waiting for us at the end of my driveway. "Is your mother still in the house?"

Colt looked frantically at the Mini Cooper he had parked behind. "That your mother's car? I'm getting outa Dodge. Listen, I just came to tell you that I reserved an hour at the indoor range – Straight Shooters Gun Shop in Manassas. Day after tomorrow, one o'clock. Can you do that?" He was running backwards, jangling his keys.

"Chicken."

"I admit it." He flapped his arms to imitate a freaky foul. "One o'clock?"

"Sure."

"Meet you there – call me if you need directions." He was in his car and gone faster than Smokey chasing The Bandit.

"Does your mother scare everyone?" Roz asked.

"No. Only my friends." The twitch was growing in intensity. I pressed a finger on the corner of my eye to stop it.

"You don't look good. Is everything okay?"

"I've been better. This throbbing headache snuck up on me about two minutes ago and it feels like there's a Mexican jumping bean under my eyelid."

"Let me get the girls for you – I'll send them up to the house. You go in and relax.

"My mother is in there. How can I relax with her around?"

Roz cut her eyes toward the top of the driveway. "Look, she's leaving now."

She was right. My mother was cramming into her spit-fire red Mini Cooper. Miraculously, she actually managed to fit her hulking frame into that tiny box. I suspected her knees knocked her chin every time she shifted gears.

"Good," I agreed. "You're right. I think I'll go lie down. Thanks."

"You'll pay me back tonight by going to that PTA meeting," Roz grinned. "I'll pick you up at seven forty-five."

My mother backed down the driveway and stopped to talk. Her window was rolled down and her sunroof opened wide. "Sweetheart. You look terrible."

"Thanks, Mom."

"Well, I hate to be the bearer of bad news, but Howard called while you were out. He said to tell you he can't stop by tonight. Something about working late." She had that you're-married-to-such-a-loser look on her face.

I sighed. "Why am I not surprised?"

"Can I give you the name and number of that single fella? He'd be a real catch."

"Fella? No one says 'fella' anymore Mom."

"You're avoiding my question."

With the nervous tick kicking in at full speed, I avoided her question real good by walking away, stomping into my house, flopping onto my lonely marital bed and letting out the bawl of the century.

Callie was a gem and cooked dinner for Amber and Bethany while I wallowed in my self-pity pit. By seven o'clock, I was on the phone with Roz trying to wheedle my way out of the PTA commitment. She'd have none of it, arguing that I should get out of the house, rather than sitting and moping about Howard. She also thought I'd get a good laugh or two from the dramatic antics and fireworks that would be unleashed in the wake of her announcement. Deciding she was probably more right than wrong, I gave Callie her babysitting instructions and stood waiting in the driveway at 6:45. Roz arrived promptly, as usual.

By 8:00 we were seated in the cushy green chairs of the Tulip Tree Elementary School library. Roz set up camp at the head of a long table and worked with exaggerated concentration on a stack of paperwork in front of her, reading, paperclipping, reading, paperclipping. I knew she was engaging herself in busy work, nervous to start the meeting and the deal with the uproar that would follow her bad news. I purposely sat several chairs away, just in case I needed to make a quick and discreet get-away.

"Is anyone sitting here?" asked a female voice.

I lifted my head to see Shashi Kapoor, the school crossing guard. Shashi was one of my favorite people at Tulip Tree. She could always be relied on for a truthful and un-edited account of happenings at the school – both in front of and behind the scenes. She had no kids of her own, but participated in school events with dedication and enthusiasm.

"Hi, Shashi. Sit down. I'd love to have you as my neighbor tonight."

Beautifully adorned in a shimmery, banana yellow sari, Shashi's bright white smile lit up the room and helped me to forget my worries.

"How are things weeth you, Barbara?" She always said my full name and enunciated every syllable.

"Fine, thanks." I smiled.

"You never come to these meetings."

"That's true."

"Roz, she brings you because she needs . . ." she looked for the right word, "moral support, eh?"

I wasn't sure how much other people knew about the yearbook debacle, so I tried to play dumb. "No. Just thought it was time. Do my part and all of that."

"Don't play dumb with me, Barbara." She smiled a wily smile. She leaned in and whispered in my ear. "I know all about thees yearbook problem. Thees meeting should be a wild one." She smiled again and elbowed me. "There's another problem there, eh?" She pointed at Michelle Alexander who sat across the table with her arms crossed and her mouth pinched tight. Granted, Michelle's grim attitude wouldn't win her Miss Congeniality, but I had no idea what Shashi was getting at. I gave her a questioning look.

"Just watch. Any second now."

As if on cue, Bunny Bergen floated in. She smiled widely. "Hi, Barb! Shashi." She was acting sane and happy, which was pretty bizarre considering the episode just hours earlier. When she saw Michelle though, her demeanor went from Jekyl to Hyde. The two women exchanged angry leers, and even though an empty chair stood next to Michelle, Bunny made a show of choosing another one farther away. She sat with exaggerated grace and shot an evil eye at Michelle.

Taken completely by surprise, I whispered to Shashi. "I thought those two were BFFs."

"They were. Thees is a new development."

"Do you know why?"

Shashi shrugged. "But I heard about Bunny's leettle trip to your house today," she said with a wink.

"News travels fast, doesn't it? She has more than a few screws loose if you ask me – I'd stay away from her if I was Michelle too." I was still bothered by Waldo's comment about Bunny being obsessed with Howard. I wanted to ask Shashi if she knew anything, but was too embarrassed.

"Well, soon enough I'll know what is wrong weeth these two. Like you say – news travels fast."

Two more women arrived and took seats at the far end of the table, then Roz called the meeting to order. Mind numbing conversation and the reading of the last minutes took more time than I liked. I fought off several yawns.

Finally, Roz took a deep breath and I knew she had no choice but to bring up the dismal topic of the sabotaged yearbook. The color had drained from her face. She cleared her throat.

The room went silent.

She took a sip of water.

Poor Roz, I thought. It was like a death walk to the gallows.

With a jolting THWAP, the double doors of the library flew open and Peggy tumbled into the room, breaking the silence and the somber mood.

"Wait!" she yelled. "Don't blame Roz! There is an answer. I've fixed everything!"

One of the women at the table asked the obvious question. "Fixed what? What needed fixing?"

"The yearbook!" smiled Peggy, very pleased with herself. She stood next to Roz now at the front of the long table. "I was thinking about it all afternoon, and it kept nagging at me. Nag, nag, nag. Then the lights clicked on – Little Kevin McIntyre!"

Roz frowned. "What?"

"Little Kevin McIntyre. Actually, he's not little anymore, he's probably, oh, six feet three or four, but we call him Little Kevin because there's a Big Kevin and we don't like to get them confused. Not that we could really get them confused, because Big Kevin died last year – undiagnosed sinus infection. Ate up his brain. It was really awful and unexpected. His wife kept telling him to go to the doctor, but he—"

Roz, sweating by now, jumped in. "Peggy! What does this have to do with the yearbook?"

"I told you. Little Kevin McIntyre. Don't you pay attention?"

Roz's jaw was locked and she spoke through gritted teeth. "WHO is Little Kevin McIntyre?"

"My cousin's – actually my cousin twice removed on my mother's side – my cousin Aurora's son. He got married just a couple of months ago and when I was at his wedding, I met his wife's sister, Judy, but everyone just calls her Jude. She's was really nice and she has three boys all the same age as mine. Our yearbook company is Time Remembered, right?"

Roz nodded, her eyes bigger than two pasta bowls. "I thought so! Jude works for them. She's an account executive." Peggy handed her a piece of paper. "That's her name and number at the office. Call her tomorrow and she'll work with you to fix everything. She said you can still have your yearbooks delivered before the end of the school year, but you HAVE to call her tomorrow."

Roz kissed the piece of paper, jumped from her chair and hugged Peggy so hard they both nearly toppled onto the floor. She didn't let go for almost a whole minute. Meanwhile, the other parents sat stupefied, unsure of what had just transpired before them.

Michelle spoke up. "What just happened?" she asked.

Roz released Peggy from her embrace. "Look at the time! Meeting adjourned. See you all next month, and thank you for coming!"

The room cleared out slowly with people leaving in twos and threes whispering about the bizarre gathering. Eventually, Roz, Peggy and I found ourselves alone in the library.

"See," I said. "You didn't need me here at all. You just needed Peggy, who, by the way seems to have missed her book club."

She waved a dismissive hand. "I was there." She raised her Cappuccino Corner cup to prove she wasn't lying. "But no one had read the book, so we set a new date and I scooted out to bring Roz the good news." She was all smiles for about two seconds. Then her shoulders drooped and she turned to me with a sad face and I-hate-to-tell-you-this eyes.

"What?" I asked.

"My news for you isn't so good." She put a hand on my shoulder. "Howard was there."

"At your book club?" Howard was of Italian heritage, but he wasn't much of a reader. I was very confused.

"No. At Cappuccino Corner." She paused. "With HER."

"The same woman we saw him with at Fiorenza's?"

Peggy nodded. "I'm sorry."

I grabbed the table for support. Pictures of Howard and the gorgeous blonde flashed through my jealous mind like a bad slide show – the two of them sipping coffee, snuggling close, staring dreamily into each other's eyes with revolting smiles on their love-infected faces. My living nightmare was interrupted by a janitor with a vacuum cleaner and a huge set of keys who shooed us out of the library telling us he had to lock up the school.

We walked to the front of the school, silent while my thoughts raced. He'd lied. He said he had to work late. He didn't love me anymore. I remembered Frankie's business card sitting on my counter at home and wondered how much money he would accept to knee-cap a traitorous spouse.

The uncomfortable lull in conversation was broken when we opened the doors and stepped out onto the sidewalk. A large parking lot spanned the entire front of the school building. At the far end, Michelle Alexander and Bunny Bergen faced-off under a street light.

"Who do you think you are?" Bunny screamed.

It was harder to hear Michelle. She was probably trying to maintain some decorum. I'm pretty sure she said, "What's your problem?" Even though it sounded like "Where's Cloris Leachman?"

"Like you don't know!"

They were too far away to see facial expressions, but we could hear Bunny's outrage just fine. Michelle was definitely on the defensive.

Bunny shoved Michelle in the chest with her index finger. "Keep your big yap shut!"

"First off," retorted Michelle, louder now, "stop shoving me!"

"It's bad enough that other people talk about me behind my back, but you're supposed to be my best friend. How would you like it if I went around telling people that you and Lance were in marriage counseling?"

"You're being paranoid, Bunny."

"Watch what you say, Miss Prissy Alexander. If I get word of you mouthing off about me again, I'll kill you. I swear I will." Bunny stalked off to her Jag. I don't know if she saw us, but Michelle did for sure. She made a movement like she might walk our way, but then turned and got into her SUV. She drove away behind Bunny, whose wheels were squealing when she peeled out.

There must have been at least one other spectator, because right after they left, the lights in a black sedan clicked on and it drove off as well.

Roz, Peggy and I stood in stunned silence, not yet ready to make a comment on the events. Finally, I couldn't help myself. I had to ask the obvious question.

"Are all PTA meetings this titillating?"

Chapter 5

Oddly, Bunny and Michelle's feline fracas in the school parking lot had lifted my spirits. Maybe I was just reveling in the knowledge that someone might have bigger problems than me, who knows? Regardless, Bunny was losing control in a big way. She'd progressed from wacko quack to super psycho freak. Of course, I still wanted to know why the FBI had been called out to her house for a mere rabbit hit and run, but I'd needle Howard for that info soon enough. Right before I castrated him.

After Roz dropped me off, I opened my front door, expecting to find things quiet with Amber in bed, Bethany reading in her room, and Callie watching TV or talking to friends on her computer.

So much for expectations. Instead, I was greeted by an unusually warm, domestic scene. Comfortably cozy on the family room sofa, my mother sat, book in hand, flanked on one side by ten year old Bethany and on the other side by six year old Amber wearing a tiger's tail and cat ears. Just two months earlier Amber had waved her fairy phase goodbye and sleuthed into her Josie and the Pussycats phase. I was going broke keeping her in DVD sets of the old cartoons, many of which she could now recite from memory.

Callie was curled up in the overstuffed comfy chair, a red blanket hiding everything except her beautiful head. Norman Rockwell could not have painted a more perfect picture himself. I touched a hand to my heart.

The girls, engrossed by the story being read to them, didn't look up as I entered. Finally, I thought, after all of these years, there was hope for my mother. She could be like other grandmothers – warm, loving and maternal.

I sat on the edge of Callie's chair and took in the literary moment, wondering what lovely, pretty little fairy tale she had chosen.

"'There isn't any night club in the world'," she read in a calm yet dramatic voice, "'you can sit in for a long time unless you can at least buy some liquor and get drunk. Or unless you're with some girl that really knocks you out.'"

I jumped to my feet. "Mom!"

She peered at me over her tortoise shell half eye glasses. "What dear?"

"What are you reading to them?"

Innocently, she turned the red paperback around so I could see the title. "*Catcher in the Rye*. It's a great American novel. You really should expose these girls to better literature. All I could find were some miserable books about that little brat on the prairie. No imagination. This, you can sink your teeth into."

I grabbed the book from her hands. "This is not appropriate! What were you thinking?"

"I was thinking that they needed exposure to art."

"Art? *Catcher in The Rye*? I'm barely comfortable with Callie hearing this stuff, but come on – Amber and Bethany?"

"This 'stuff' as you so blithely dismiss it, is considered some of the most important writing of the twentieth century. I'm taking a college literature course – reconnecting with the classics. You know, I dated JD for a brief time."

Again, with a big fish tale.

"You dated JD Salinger?" Suspicion was evident in my tone.

"It was a long time ago," she said, adding a nonchalant wave of her hand. "Before I met your father."

Everything my mother claimed to have done in her life, including an ambiguous stint on Broadway, auditioning for the role of Bond girl, and getting drunk with Ernest Hemingway, happened before she met my father. Since she would never confess to her real age, I figured she was either a very precocious teenager, or she met my father when she was sixty.

"Mom, JD Salinger was a recluse."

"Only after we dated."

If her story was true, Salinger's fear of people was finally explained.

She exhausted me. The woman simply exhausted me. More than anything, I just wanted to crawl into bed and put the horrible day behind me. I looked at my watch.

"Mom, it's ten o'clock. Amber and Bethany should have been asleep over an hour ago." I waved in the direction of the stairs. "Go girls. Get up there now."

"We want more! Please, Mom?"

"You heard me – up there now." Reluctantly and with the speed of two sloths, they did as I asked, Amber dragging her sad tiger tail behind her.

"Callie, you too. Shoo!" Callie performed the required teenage eye roll. She was a skilled eye-roller. Almost as good as her father.

"Why me?" she wailed as the eyeballs spun. "I'm not a baby."

"I'm sure Grandma has somewhere important she has to be. Hang gliding lessons? Bungee jumping off Memorial Bridge? Climbing Mount Everest maybe?"

A skilled master at initiating awkward moments, my mom stared me down without giving up an answer. Silent seconds ticked away. Sweat beaded on my forehead. Callie wiggled restlessly then snuck silently away. When the Grand Intimidator had achieved the desired effect, she spoke.

"Actually," she pulled the tortoise shell frames slowly from her face. "I will be going momentarily. I expect my ride any second now."

I wondered why she would need a ride until it hit me – her Mini Cooper wasn't in the driveway when I got home.

The doorbell rang.

Intuition and experience told me she was up to something.

Her eyes lit up like Roman candles on the Fourth of July. "There he is now!"

He? Either she had a boyfriend or . . . before I could consider the alternative, she shot out of her chair and leapt to the door. She was amazingly agile for a woman with such large bone mass. Something akin to the progeny of a gazelle and a wooly mammoth.

"Russ! Come in. I'll get my things." She was gushing.

Poking my head around the corner, a vision of supreme studliness befell my weary eyes.

She dragged me into the foyer. "Barbara, meet my friend, Russell Crow."

I laughed.

Russell smiled.

"I get that all the time," he responded with a half-chuckle. "Spelled C-R-O-W though. No E on the end." Russell smiled real nice.

"Oh, who needs that E anyway?" I blabbered while soaking in his six-foot plus, plentifully abbed-frame, wavy blonde hair and deliciously rugged but blemish-free skin. He was a god. An Adonis. A godly Adonis had walked into my house in little old Rustic Woods,Virginia. My heart skipped about twenty beats.

"Russell is a fire fighter at the station just down the road. I met him at my Citizen's Fire Fighter Academy."

Of course, he was a fire fighter. They're all hunks. It's true – go to a station sometime and just try to find a fat and ugly fireman. They don't exist. I couldn't help from smiling.

"He's the single fella I mentioned earlier," my mother added.

My smile fell, my heart stalled, and my face flushed frantic fuschia.

While I quickly pondered very specific and merciless methods for murdering the woman who supposedly gave me life, Russell squelched the flames of my embarrassment by offering his hand for a shake, "You can call me Russ," he said. "And don't let your mother worry you. I'm not married, but I am seeing someone."

"Thank goodness, because I'm married! I mean, not that if you weren't married . . . I mean . . . well if I weren't married . . . do you have a gun? A cross-bow? Because if you did, I'd ask you to end my misery right now."

Russell Crow's feathers didn't ruffle even a wee bit. He continued smiling, unfazed by my incoherent dithering. "No worries. We have to get going." He put his hand up for a farewell wave. "It was nice meeting you."

"You too," I managed to squeak while shooting deadly daggers of doom toward my mother who scooted out the door.

Before the door closed behind them, I heard Russell yell. "I've got it now!"

The door opened and Russell's dreamy head appeared.

"You've got what now?" I asked.

"Where I've seen you before."

"You've seen me before?"

"Were you over on Green Ashe Place earlier today? Talking with an FBI agent?"

I nodded.

"I thought so. I never forget a face. Especially such a pretty one."

I gulped. "That agent was my husband, Howard."

"He's a lucky man." He pulled his head back out and closed my door.

Holy cow. Talk about combustion. Fires were ignited in regions that hadn't been ablaze for some time. A cold shower was in order. I was a married woman, after all.

Upstairs, Amber laid in bed with covers up to her chin, cat ears still in place, and awaiting her goodnight kiss. We rubbed noses.

"Mommy, what's a prom?"

"It's a special high school dance. Why?"

"Callie is being a grouchy pants and Bethany says it's 'cuz she's hoping Brandon will ask her to the prom, but he hasn't yet."

I smiled. "That makes sense." Brandon had been around our house a few times and I wondered if Callie was hoping for more than friendship.

"Not to me it doesn't. Does that mean that she wants to kiss him? If it does, then that's just plain yucky." She stuck out her tongue. "Samuel Tinker said he wanted to kiss me on the playground and I told him if he tried, I'd punch him in his peanuts."

"Where did you hear that word?"

"Emily Barnes. Why? Is it a bad word?"

"It depends on where you think his peanuts are . . . located."

"In his stomach. Where else?"

"Good. Well, from now on, just call a stomach, a stomach. To avoid misunderstandings."

"Why would there be any missed understandings?"

"Trust me."

She sighed. "I don't want to grow up, thank you very much."

"Why?"

"You people seem to make everything way too complicaketed."

"Complicated."

"See what I mean?"

We exchanged kisses and I turned out the light.

Bethany's room was dark, but I could see a flashlight under her covers. The girl lived to read.

"Good night, Bethy."

"'Night Mom."

"Promise you'll turn the flashlight off before eleven?"

"Sure, Mom."

I found Callie at her desk in front of the computer, her fingers dancing furiously on the keyboard. She'd pulled her thick, walnut hair off her shoulders with a band.

"Hey, gorgeous," I said, sitting on the edge of her bed.

She didn't look up. "Hey."

"Whatcha doin'?"

"Homework." Her fingers kept typing.

I traced little blue flowers on her bedspread. "Oh."

"Do you want something?"

"No." I cleared my throat while I looked around her room. "Not really."

"That's a Grandma move."

It mortified me that she was right. "I was just wondering . . ."

She stopped what she was doing and turned her head to peer at me with an annoyed expression. "Mom."

"Has anyone asked you to the prom yet?"

"There's more to that question, isn't there?"

"I don't know . . . is there?"

"What's with the vague-speak?"

"I was just trying to communicate in your own language. Isn't that how teens talk? Stepping around the real issue, but everyone knows what you're talking about?"

"In your day maybe. Teens have evolved since the sixteenth century. Now we just come out and ask. It's much easier that way."

"Touché." She was a witty one and I couldn't help but grin. "Well, from one decaying, primeval mother to one progressive, worldly teenager: has Brandon asked you to the prom yet?"

The corners of her mouth tugged reluctantly into a pretty smile and she shook her head. "Not yet."

"Not yet?" I was tingly with excitement for her. "But you think he's going to ask?"

"I think so. He keeps showing up out of no where and acts sort of weird. And he texts me like fifty times a day."

I nodded. "That's a sure sign. He'll get up the courage soon enough. You just let me know when we need to go dress shopping, okay?"

I kissed her forehead. "Go to bed at a decent hour, would you?"

By eleven-thirty, I had seen all three girls to bed, taken a shower, sipped a half-glass of wine and cried a tear or two over Howard and his new woman. I only allowed myself two tears though. The crying and moping was going to stop pronto. No more whining. I crawled into bed and concluded that tomorrow was a new day. I wasn't ready to be a divorcee. I loved my husband. True, there were many handsome and eligible men out there like Fire Fighter Russell Crow, but it seemed to me that a George Clooney in the bush was better than two Russell Crows in the hand.

With that, the decision to win back my husband was made and I turned out my light, calm and resolute in declaring war at the break of dawn.

Then the phone rang.

I groped for the receiver. Unidentifiable items clinked and clanked as they hit my floor in my failed attempt to answer the call before it woke up the household. Finally, my hands landed on the cordless receiver. I clicked the "talk" button, hopeful Howard would be on the other end. "Hello?"

So much for hope.

"Barb?" The female voice was familiar, but I couldn't place it at first.

"Yeah. . ."

"Can you come over? I'm sick."

"Bunny? Is that you?"

"Yes. It's just so awful. Can you come?"

"Well . . . I just got into bed. Don't you have . . . you know – friends you could call?"

"I don't have any friends. Not anymore."

"Bunny . . ."

"Please Barb! I need someone right now. I'm . . . I'm scared." She seemed to be slurring her words. Even I was a little worried for her.

"Fine. I'll be there in a few minutes. I need to get dressed."

A dial tone in my ears was the only response.

"Bunny?"

Dial tone.

Damn! I slammed the phone down.

I turned on my light and slipped a pair of sweats over my pajama bottoms, then peeked out my window at Roz's house. I didn't want to go to Bunny's alone. That woman was one fry short of a Happy Meal. Reinforcements were needed. Thankfully, Roz's bedroom light shone brightly. She was probably reading. I reached for the phone and dialed her number.

"What's wrong?" she answered on the first ring.

"I know it's late. Sorry. I just got this weird call from Bunny. She says she's scared and wants me to come over."

"Doesn't she have any friends to call?"

"I already asked that question."

"And?"

"She says she doesn't have any friends anymore."

"After tonight, I guess that's no surprise."

"My thoughts exactly. I'm not going over there alone. She threatened to kill Michelle after all."

"Now you're just being silly. She only said that in the heat of the moment."

"I won't go if you don't come with me."

"Fine. You drive."

"I'll be right over."

I checked on the girls and taped a note to my bedroom door just in case any of them woke up while I was gone and came looking for me. I put on my jacket and tapped the pocket to make sure my cell phone was there. Check. Finally, I slipped on a pair of clogs, picked up my keys and exited the house as quietly as possible, locking the door behind me.

The air had grown chilly and I shivered as I crawled into my car. After a minute of fiddling to get the key into the ignition, I turned the engine over, shattering the dark silence of the night with its oil-deprived roar.

A knock on the passenger's window startled me until I realized it was Roz. She opened the door and slipped in. "Thought I'd save you the long drive to my house," she said smiling.

"I'm glad you're so chipper at this late hour."

Determined to make this strange call of the wild short and sweet, I threw the gear shift into reverse, backed out and sped toward the stop sign at the end of White Willow Circle.

Roz white-knuckled her armrest. "It's a mini-van, Barb. Not a Ferrari."

"Sorry." I looked both ways for a safe turn onto Tall Birch Avenue. "I just want to get this over with."

"Be careful. We've got all night."

One of my biggest gripes about Rustic Woods was the No Street Lights rule. Supposedly the issue was "light pollution." I grumbled often and made several complaints to the homeowners association, as did other residents, to no avail. My headlights barely made a dent in the dense blackness of the moonless night. However, it was late, and there wasn't another set of headlights anywhere around, so I turned left. We'd be at Bunny's in less than a minute.

I couldn't get Bunny's odd behavior out of my mind and was about to ask Roz what she thought, when she shouted. "Barb, watch out!"

I hit the brakes, but not before I heard the thump.

My neck ached from stopping so fast. "What happened?"

"You hit something."

"What?"

"I don't know. It's too dark. I saw something out of the corner of my eye. A deer maybe?"

"I never saw a deer."

"Well you hit something!"

"Okay, okay. Calm down. I'll get out and check." Shifting back to park and leaving the engine idling, I opened my door. My feet landed on the street rather than a dead animal, so things were looking up. I ran my fingers along the front side of my van – no dents. Another good sign. No front bumper damage either as far as I could tell and nothing on the ground in front. Maybe Roz was wrong. Maybe I hadn't hit anything. I continued along the front bumper when it became very obvious that Roz was right. Well, she was sort of right. I hadn't hit something.

I had hit someone.

Michelle Alexander.

Chapter 6

Roz opened the door when I started shrieking.

"No!" I yelled. "You'll step on her! Crawl through the driver's side."

She scrambled across while I knelt by Michelle's body. The beams from my headlights didn't offer a ton of visibility since she was sprawled on the ground beside my van rather than in front of it, but there was enough light to see the face of my victim. My mind swirled at the possibility that I had just killed someone. Barbara Marr: Mother Killer. My unflattering mug shot would be plastered across every newscast and newspaper in the DC Metro area. People would point at the picture and ask, "Is that Charles Manson?" "No," others would respond. "That's The Mother Killer – Barbara Marr. Hope she fries." My daughters would have to hang their heads in shame in school while I sat in a cold jail cell and learned to play the harmonica.

Of course, I would only be a murderer if she was actually dead. Jumping to conclusions of her demise wasn't fair to anyone. Taking precious seconds to calm my erratic respiration and faster-than-the speed-of-light pulse, I crawled closer to her face. I recalled a CPR course I had taken with my mother a few years earlier. Check for breathing. There was something about checking for breathing. How hard could that be?

I put my face even with her chest and tried to see if it rose and fell, but my eyeballs were actually pulsing, if that's possible, so everything seemed to be moving. Probably some horrible curse of accidental mother murderers. Homicidal Eyeball Pulsing Syndrome. I would have to ask my optometrist about that.

"Who is it?" Roz asked. She was behind me now.

"Michelle Alexander. I think she's dead! Do you have your cell phone?"

"I forgot it!"

I reached in my jacket pocket for my own, but pulled out Bethany's Game Boy instead. I felt in my other pocket. No cell phone. Damn! "Run back to the house and call 911!"

Roz was gone in a flash.

Since the look-see test wasn't working, I decided I should feel near her nose for any sign of breathing. Only, I was breathing heavier than a hormone-heavy teenage boy at a cheerleader convention. I couldn't tell if the breath was hers or mine.

Then she moaned and coughed a bit.

I probably broke all sorts of rules about moving accident victims, yada, yada, yada, but I wasn't thinking clearly and I was just so thankful that she was alive that I lifted her head off the ground.

"Michelle?"

No response except a small rattle in her breathing. When I put my hand on her chest, it felt wet and warm. I assumed that was blood, but it was just too hard to tell. The moment called for a flashlight. Remembering that I had one in my van, I started to put her head back down so I could retrieve it. She moaned again.

"Michelle?"

I thought she was trying to talk, but it was hard to tell.

"Michelle? Do you want to say something?"

She moved her head in what might have been interpreted as a nod.

"Michelle. I'm so sorry – I didn't see you—"

She gurgled and spat up some blood.

"Hang on. Roz went to call 911. Help should be here soon." I rocked her a little.

"Poo," she said, barely audible.

"What?"

"Poo," she coughed. She grabbed my arm and pulled her head close to mine. She looked me in the eyes. "Pooh Bear."

"Pooh Bear? Is that what you're trying to say?"

She nodded and closed her eyes. Seconds later, she went completely limp. I screamed again. Michelle Alexander had just died in my arms. I'd killed her. My head swam and without thinking I jumped up and started running.

The problem was, I ran right into a low-hanging tree limb. A big one.

I'm in a room without light. In the darkness, I hear a voice.

"Barb? Barb? Are you okay?"

The voice is familiar. I realize the room isn't dark – my eyes are closed. I'm desperately drowsy as if I've been drugged. My eyes don't seem to want to open.

"Meryl? Is that you?"

When times get tough, two people tend to find their way into my world of dreams – the ever sexy Lord of Great Movies, Steven Spielberg, and the one true Goddess of the Cinema, Meryl Streep. I mean really, if you're gonna dream, dream big, right?

Desperate to see Meryl Streep, I struggle, but eventually manage to pry my eyes open. She's a vision standing above me awash in a luminous glow. Her hair bounces gently, as if swept by a soft breeze. But there is no breeze. It's just her goddess-ness that makes her so wispy and willowy.

"Barb. It's time." She has the voice of an angel.

Still holding my eyes open with my fingers, I apologize for not understanding her.

"Time for what, Meryl?"

"To win another Oscar. Will you write my award winning screenplay? I have a title in mind – The Patient Englishman in Africa."

I don't know how to answer. I've never written a screenplay before. "I'm not sure—"

"We'll have your husband play the romantic lead."

"Howard?"

"He looks like George Clooney, does he not?"

Before I can protest her poor casting choice, Meryl transforms before my pried-open eyes. She's blonde, but she's not Meryl anymore. There is something about her I recognize. The perfect makeup and nails. The body that won't stop. She saunters toward me. It's a proud and pompous saunter.

"I know you!" I scream. "You're Fiorenza's Floozy!"

She flips her hair and smooths her tight, barely-below-the-unmentionables short skirt. Howard appears out of nowhere. He walks up behind Fiorenza's Floozy and kisses the back of her neck. His hands caress her body. Floozy moans and groans.

"Howard!" I scream, hyperventilating. "We're still married. What are you doing?"

He lifts his head. "She's sexy. What do you want me to do? Ignore my natural impulses?" He returns to Floozie's neck.

"I'll get sexy."

Howard laughs and takes another break from practically devouring Floozy altogether. "Get real. You haven't worn a pair of heels in ten years. You never wear skirts or dresses. You probably don't even have a push-up bra."

"I . . . I don't have anything to push up." I look down at my sad excuse for a chest. It's true. Nursing three babies has sucked the life right out of my once proud and perky friends. Whereas Floozy is sporting a pair of well-crafted and outrageously expensive melons, on a good day my own breasts barely resemble two dehydrated garbanzo beans.

I love Meryl Streep, but she's gone and I want this nightmare to end.

A scream pierces my eardrum.

My scalp throbbed. I opened my eyes. Strobing red lights cut the shroud of darkness and siren screams pierced the quiet air of our once sleeping neighborhood. Flat on my back, I reached up to feel my wet forehead.

"Don't touch," said Roz. "The ambulance just pulled up – a medic should be over here in a second."

I attempted to sit despite the aches in my body. "Roz, while you were gone, Michelle . . ." I couldn't bring myself to say the words.

"They're with her now."

"I think I killed her." My face puckered and the tears started flowing. The crying made my head hurt worse. It was all such an awful nightmare. I wiped my wet face and nose with my shirt sleeve. "Where's Howard?" I sniffled. "Did you call Howard?"

"He wasn't home, but Colt's on his way. The police are trying to reach Howard now, I think."

More sniffling. "Thanks."

"Here's comes the medic," said Roz. "I'm going to go ask Mrs. Perkins to stay in your house just in case the girls wake up. Mrs. Perkins lived on our street. She loved me until I found a body-less head in the basement of another house on our street, inadvertently opening up a Pandora's box of neighborhood secrets involving dead undercover cops and the Mafia. Simple mistake, really. But, mistake or not, Mrs. Perkins didn't like me so much after that. It had taken me months to regain her trust. Running down and killing an innocent mother on a nighttime stroll was probably going to roll me back several points on the trust-o-meter.

"Can't *you* stay with the girls?" I asked, taking another swipe to dry away tears.

"They want me here to answer questions. I'll be back in a minute to check on you."

Police had erected poles with lamps that lit up the area like daytime. A young man in a blue jacket knelt beside me.

"Ma'am, my name is Juan. I'm going to take care of you. Can you tell me your name and what happened?"

Through mini-sobs and lingering sniffles, I told Juan the EMT my sad story about hitting Michelle Alexander and my subsequent encounter with the rogue tree limb while running for help. He listened patiently as I blubbered, while feeling my arms and legs, moving them gently. He nodded when I was done speaking.

"I don't think you have any broken bones. Can you walk to the ambulance? I want to check your blood sugar level and take your blood pressure."

I nodded. "You're very nice, Juan. Thank you. If it turns out I'm a killer, will you still be nice to me?"

"I'm sure you're not a killer, Mrs. Marr." He smiled.

He offered his assistance in walking to the ambulance and was kind enough to guide me around the scene where emergency responders hovered over Michelle's body.

Colt's red GTO slid quickly beside the ambulance just as Juan was helping me in.

"Curly," he said, barely letting the car come to a complete stop before leaping out.

"Hi," I tried to smile. "Wanna join me? It's warmer in here." I had settled down considerably, and seeing Colt, his face tight with concern, raised my spirits.

He jumped into the back of the ambulance nearly toppling poor Juan while he wrapped the blood pressure cuff around my arm. The other EMT, a young woman, did not seem pleased with Colt's presence.

"Uh, sir . . ." she said, putting her hand up as if to ward him off.

I stopped her short. No one was going to turn Colt away at a time like this.

"No. Please let him stay. He's my friend."

Colt, ignoring the woman altogether, had already knelt in front of me and wrapped my hands tightly in his own. They were warm and strong and sent a force of energy so powerful through every fiber of my body that I nearly forgot my dire circumstances entirely.

The lady EMT gave up her argument without a fight.

He brushed a couple of curls from my eyes. "Are you okay?"

"Define okay. I don't have any broken bones. Is that okay? Did they tell you what happened?"

"I got the gist."

"I killed a woman. She was still breathing when Roz went to call 911, then—" I shivered and felt sick to my stomach again.

Colt tipped my chin so I would be forced to look him in the eyes. "We don't know what happened yet. I'll get some answers." He looked at Juan the EMT. "What's your plan here?"

"Her blood pressure is a little low," he said. "And we're concerned about a concussion. We'll be transporting her to Rustic Woods Hospital for observation."

"Don't leave without me," Colt demanded with a stern finger point. "I'll see what I can find out and be right back." Colt kissed me on the forehead and jumped down, walking with determined confidence toward the nearest policeman.

"Colt!" I yelled. He turned back. "Ask them if they found Howard."

Things happened quickly after that. Roz came to tell me Mrs. Perkins would stay with the girls until my mother arrived. I asked Roz why she had to call my mother and Roz said who else would she call? A burly policeman with a generous pair of eye brows told me he had some questions to ask. He fired away while Juan pricked my finger to collect blood. What time did you leave your house? Where were you going? Who was with you in the car? Did you see the victim before you hit her? Did you hear anyone scream or yell when you hit the victim? Did you ingest legal or illegal drugs? Were you drinking alcoholic beverages this evening?

I could feel the blood drain further from my extremities with each question, so it was no surprise when Juan had to apologize and grab yet another finger to attack. I felt like a pincushion being interrogated on a bad episode of *NYPD Blue*.

Being sequestered inside the ambulance prevented me from observing exterior events, but I did hear a sharp, single siren followed by some bustling and an obscenity or two. The cop straightened and pulled his gut in as far as it would go. Somebody important had arrived.

"Sir," he said with a nod to the as yet unseen arrival.

"Officer," replied the voice.

My heart jumped. I knew that voice.

Howard's head appeared around the corner of the ambulance bay. His grim face lightened when he saw me, allowing a somber but gentle smile to appear. Jumping inside, he grabbed me in a hug and held on tight. He was warm and I was in heaven.

After a long and loving embrace, he pulled back. "How do you feel?"

"I'm fine. It may be a while before I can use these again," I said, holding up my three band-aided fingertips. "But they say I should be back to normal in no time – ready to get behind the wheel and mow down any innocent mother who gets in my way." My voice cracked. The witty attempt to forget my problems backfired. The tears that had retreated earlier made a valiant comeback.

Another commotion erupted outside the ambulance. The burly cop had tried to stop a passerby from getting into the fray. Only it was no ordinary passerby. It was my mother.

"What do you mean I have to leave? I will do no such thing. Just who do you think you're talking to? Where's my daughter?"

True, the cop was round and sturdy, but he was no match for my mother who had a good three to four inches on him. Not to mention the venomous disposition of a cobra.

She pushed him out of her way and marched toward me. She frowned when she spied Howard.

"Howard," she said, acknowledging his presence.

"Diane."

"I was told you were nowhere to be found."

"Evidently you were told wrong."

"How are they treating my daughter?" she asked. Apparently, she wasn't expecting an answer because she continued right on without a break for air. "How are they treating you dear? Did they take your blood pressure?" She looked at Juan. "What's her blood pressure? Are her pupils dilated?" Back to me: "They should take you to the hospital for observation." To Juan again: "Are you taking her to the hospital for observation?"

"Mom, calm down. I'm fine. They know what they're doing."

"How do you know? I'm registered in emergency care – these are the kinds of questions I always ask in situations like this."

"You're not an EMT."

"I said I was registered in emergency care."

"That was a CPR course."

"I'm registered."

"To do CPR."

Juan chimed in. "How long ago did you do that course?"

"Three, four years ago."

"Then your registration has expired. Step away from my vehicle."

Howard jumped out of the ambulance and landed next to my stupefied mother.

"Diane, can you take the girls to your condo for the night? I need to stay here and wrap things up."

"You can't come with me to the hospital?" I whined.

"I'll try. I want to stick around in case I'm needed for media control being that you're an FBI agent's wife. They eat that stuff up. I'll get there when I can."

"I can take the girls," she said.

"Did you come in your car?" I asked her.

"Of course."

"You can't fit all three girls in that ridiculous toy of a car. Howard, that won't work."

"I'll drive them to her place," offered Colt, who had magically appeared next to Howard. "Hey Howie," he said elbowing Howard playfully.

Howard stared Colt down.

"Sorry," Colt corrected himself like a scolded teenager. "Agent Marr."

"Thank you," said Howard. "You help Diane get the girls and their things. Bring them out the back door so they see as little as possible. I'll find Roz and see if she can ride to the hospital with Barb."

"Yes, sir!" said Colt with a salute.

"Coltrane Amadeus Baron," chided my mother, "Won't you ever grow up?"

"Growing up is for sissies. It's much more challenging to nurture the child within."

With a harumpf, my mother marched off to the house. Colt gave me a shrug and a wink as he hollered after her. "Meetcha there in a minute with the car Diane!"

When they were gone, I pleaded with Howard. "I feel fine – I don't need to go to the hospital. Tell them to let me stay here."

"They know what they're doing and they want to observe you for a few hours. I'll get there when I can."

"Howard?"

"Yeah?"

"Why couldn't you come for dinner tonight?

"Didn't Diane give you the message? I had to work."

"Peggy saw you working with that sleazy tramp at Cappuccino Corner."

He didn't blink. He didn't speak either.

"The same one I saw you with at Fiorenza's last night."

He blinked once but he still didn't speak.

Roz broke the silence.

"Colt said you were looking for me."

Howard jumped at the chance to change the subject. "Can you go with Barb to the hospital? I have to stay here on the scene."

"Sure. Let me run to the house, tell Peter and grab a couple of things."

She scampered away, leaving Howard and I staring silently at each other. A police officer broke the tension when he tapped Howard on the shoulder and pulled him aside for a whispered discussion. Meanwhile the other ambulance screamed off with sirens blaring.

"What was that about?" I asked after the officer left.

"The victim."

"Her name is Michelle Alexander."

He seemed surprised. "You know her?"

"Of course," I said. "She lives around the corner. Her kids go to Tulip Tree Elementary."

"Really? Well, she's alive."

"Thank God." I felt ready to cry again, but from relief this time.

"She's barely hanging on though. They're transporting her to Fairfax Hospital – they have a better trauma center than Rustic Woods. It wasn't your impact that injured her, Barb. They figure you only tapped her at most."

"I don't understand."

"Someone shot her. One bullet barely missed her heart as far as they can tell."

"One bullet – how many times was she shot?"

"Three times. At close range." He shook his head. "It's a miracle she's still alive."

Chapter 7

Chills rippled down my spine while little hairs jumped to attention on the nape of my clammy neck. Suddenly, this had become a totally different game of ball. I didn't waste Michelle like a pro-bowler taking down ten pins in a strike. Someone had been playing a deadly round of lead marbles with her long before Roz and I came along. Poor Michelle. Who would do such a thing? If we hadn't been heading out to Bunny's . . . uh oh. Bunny Bergen. Of course! And Roz said I was being silly about her threatening to kill Michelle.

"Barb? You okay?" Howard's voice shocked me back to the present.

"Howard – it was Bunny."

"What?"

"They had a fight – Bunny and Michelle – tonight after the PTA meeting. She even said she'd kill her. And that's why Roz and I were going out so late. Bunny called me to come over. She probably shot her in some heated moment of passion and then regretted it. Or maybe she didn't regret it. Maybe we were next. I knew she was insane. You need to send people over there right now!"

Howard shook his head. "It's a police matter. The FBI isn't involved."

"But you can tell them about Bunny, right?"

"I . . ." he hesitated. "I can't talk about this."

"Why were you at her house this morning anyway? What's going on with Bunny Bergen? You know something."

"I told you I can't talk about this."

Roz popped up, holding up a pair of keys in her hand. "I'm ready. I thought it would be better if I followed in my own car. Then we have a way home if they release you. That okay with you?"

I didn't want to let the topic go. "Howard?"

He wasn't budging. "You need to go."

Bewildered, Roz glanced between us. "Did anyone hear what I said?"

Fine. If Howard didn't care that Bunny Bergen was running around assassinating the mothers of Rustic Woods, then neither did I. "Sure, Roz. That's a good idea. Juan will keep me company, right Juan?"

Juan smiled while wrapping things up for our departure.

"I'll call you to check in," Howard said, putting his hand on mine.

"Sure. You go do your job."

"Barb – I love you. We'll talk about. . . that other thing later."

"Bunny?"

"No. The OTHER, other thing."

Juan, as wonderful as he was, interrupted Howard at the absolutely wrong moment. "Time to go."

Howard stepped away, the doors swung closed, the siren whooped, and we were off.

True to her word, Roz followed right on our tail and walked alongside my gurney as the EMTs wheeled me through the emergency entrance at Rustic Woods Hospital. After I answered a gazillion questions, they rolled me into a curtained area where the checked my blood pressure and tested my pupils for dilation. People kept coming and going. Roz and I didn't have enough privacy to talk to Roz about Michelle, the gunshot wounds, or Bunny. Could Bunny be crazy enough to attempt murder? I wondered whether Roz had said anything to the police about her.

"Mrs. Marr, a doctor will be here soon. Lie back and relax." The gray-haired, spectacled nurse pulled the curtain behind her, finally leaving Roz and me alone.

Roz scooted her little stool to the side of my bed, her eyes wide in curiosity. "Did Howard tell you anything?"

"Michelle is alive, did you know that?"

"Yes. I'm so relieved."

"Do you know she was walking around with three gunshot wounds when I hit her?"

"No!"

I nodded. "Howard says I barely tapped her. They can't believe she's still alive – whoever shot her really wanted her DOA."

Roz's jaw dropped. "That's awful. I guess it's lucky that Bunny called you. We wouldn't have been out otherwise. Who knows what would have happened?"

"Lucky? Or planned event? Roz. Aren't you following the dots here?"

She rolled her eyes. I was really tired of people rolling their eyes at me. I'm not as stupid as I look. "Roz. Think. Bunny shows up on my lawn looney as a tune. Then the entire Rustic Woods fire and rescue brigade descends on her house – just because she ran over a rabbit? Really? I'm not buying it. Then she threatens Michelle in broad daylight—"

"It was night time."

"In broad nightlight – says she'll kill her – then, as the song goes, 'isn't it ironic?' Michelle shows up filled with more holes than a bag of lifesavers. AND whose phone call caused me to get me to get in my car and ultimately hit Michelle? Hmm?"

Roz crossed her arms. "That song has nothing to do with irony."

"Would you stay on topic here?"

"I don't get what one thing has to do with the other."

"You mean, that she threatens to kill Michelle and then Michelle ends up almost killed?"

"No – I mean I don't know what this morning's event has to do with the other thing."

"You mean, that she has a mondo bizarro meltdown, then threatens to kill Michelle, then Michelle ends up almost killed? That thing?"

"Okay – you made your point." She crossed her arms. "It's suspicious."

"Thank you." I blew some dangling hair out of my face. "And yet, Howard doesn't think so."

"What do you mean?"

"I told Howard about their fight after the PTA. He didn't want to talk about it."

"Well, that is a little strange. Something else too, now that I think of it."

"About Bunny?"

"No – back at the accident scene. When the police questioned me, they asked basic questions, like why we were out, where we were going, whether you'd been drinking. Things you'd expect them to ask. But, if they knew she'd been shot, why didn't they ask me if I'd seen anything suspicious?"

I silently wondered the same thing. "Me too," I said finally. "Same questions."

"They questioned your mom too."

"Why?"

"Well, I don't think they questioned her so much as she gave them a load of information they may or may not have wanted. Evidently there was some man at your house with her after the PTA meeting."

"Russell Crow."

"Who?"

"Not the actor – the fire fighter."

"Yum."

"Trust me. He's as good as they get."

"Muscles?"

"Sculpted like a DaVinci original."

"Five o'clock shadow?"

"Sensationally sexy stubble."

"Wow. At your house?"

"My mother is trying to set me up with him."

"You're married."

"She thinks that's negotiable. So does Howard I guess."

"Anyway," Roz said, "I did mention that we were on our way to Bunny Bergen's house, since they asked where we were going. So Howard won't be looking into her as a suspect?"

"He said it's a police matter. The FBI isn't involved."

She ran her hands through her hair. "Well, I'm tired. I just want to get home and forget that any of this happened." The phone in her hand rang, startling us both. She looked at the display. "Peggy."

Just as Roz answered, a lady doctor pulled the curtain back. "Cell phones aren't allowed in the hospital. You'll need to take that outside."

"Peggy, I'll call you back."

Roz left while the lady introduced herself as Dr. Vaziri then gave me the once over for the umpteenth time.

"How's your head, Mrs. Marr?"

"It's sore where the branch hit," I said, touching my bandaged forehead. "Otherwise, it's fine."

"I see no reason to admit you. You don't show signs of concussion or swelling. They brought you in because you lost consciousness when you took that blow to your head, but that may have been due to the mental trauma of the other accident. I suggest you go home and rest. Make sure someone stays with you for at least twenty-four hours."

I didn't tell her that my chances of keeping that promise were iffy at best.

Roz drove us home while I talked to Peggy on her cell.

"She was shot?" asked Peggy.

"Three times."

"How is she?"

"I don't know. Howard says she's lucky to be alive – the shots were at close range."

"I'll stop by her house tomorrow and see if I can help her husband in any way. He's such a nice guy."

"How well do you know Michelle?"

"She goes to my church and her boys come over to play sometimes. This is just awful. How are you?"

"Tired. Can we finish talking tomorrow?"

"Si, Signora. I'll talk to you both after I run my morning errands."

The clock on Roz's dash read 2:31 a.m. when we pulled onto White Willow Circle. The neighborhood was void of law enforcement and emergency vehicles. All signs of turmoil were gone. So was my van. Howard's car was parked on the street though. Roz wanted to walk me up to the front door, but I insisted that she just let me out in the driveway. I might have run over a dying woman and tried to decapitate myself with a tree limb, but I wasn't an invalid.

Chapter 8

Seeing Howard's car parked out front had brightened my mood. I hadn't been surprised that he didn't make it to the hospital. His work always took him longer than he predicted. It was the curse of being an FBI wife. More often than not, two hours could become two days or even two weeks.

Expecting to find him in the house, I searched each room quickly. He wasn't downstairs, so I leaped up several stairs at a time while calling his name, fully certain he'd be in our bed, waiting to welcome me home with a kiss and a hug and other displays of affection worthy of an R rating. Maybe if I was really lucky, X rated activities would follow.

So much for censored fun. He was nowhere to be found. For good measure, I checked each of the girls' rooms, but Howard was a missing entity. It seemed odd that his car was home and he wasn't, but I was just too tired and achy to think about it anymore. My body needed a bed to lie down on. My mind needed sleep. Back in the husband-free room, I sat on the edge of the bed, slipped off one shoe then the other and let myself fall back. I'd strip down and get into some jammies in a minute, after giving the ol' eyeballs a momentary rest . . .

I'm at the Cannes Film Festival. I'm there to review selected screenings but am driving down a seaside road in my van looking for a place to park. Crowds of A-list stars cover the sidewalks while paparazzi swarm like ants at a celebrity picnic. It's a dream within a dream. Without warning, I lose control of the van – it's driving itself and there's nothing I can do. It swerves fast to the right, then again fast to the left. People are screaming and running every which way.

"Get out of my way!" I holler. "I'm a menace behind the wheel! They should revoke my license!"

Now I realize the van has turned into a Mini Cooper and Matt Damon is sitting next to me.

"Drive it like I did in the Bourne Identity," he says.

"But Matt, that wasn't you – that was a stunt driver."

He looks upset. "Really? Oh, Pooh Bear."

Before I know it, Matt is gone and Winnie-the-Pooh sits in his place eating from a honey jar.

"Pooh Bear," I say to myself. "Why does that sound so familiar?"

When I look up, the Mini-Cooper is about to plow right into the entire cast of Porky's Revenge.

My eyes opened before I witnessed the pigs fly.

Pooh Bear. Michelle's last words before she lost consciousness. In all of the mayhem, I'd forgotten. Was it a message? Like Orson Wells whispering "Rosebud" just before he dropped the snowglobe then kicked the bucket in *Citizen Kane*? Or did she just have a thing for silly ol' bears? My head started to pound as I relived the grisly scene from last night. I touched the throbbing spot and felt a nasty knot where the tree branch had struck me. Wouldn't I be a lovely sight? The clock on my bed stand told me it was 7:05 in the morning. Not exactly a full night's restful sleep, but I was awake now and sounds drifted from downstairs. Someone was home.

When I pulled the quilt away to sit up, I remembered I had fallen asleep uncovered. Then I noticed the note on the bed next to me. *Shower before you come down. You don't want to scare the girls. Came up with a story – just play along.* The handwriting wasn't Howard's – it was Colt's familiar scrawl. What a guy. It wasn't until I looked in the mirror that I understood why the girls might become frightened. My shirt and sweatpants were stained with blood. Some dried caked remnants remained on my arms as well, even though they tried to clean it off at the hospital.

The shower felt so good that I didn't want it to end. But taking up residence in the bathroom was no way to live, so I got out, dressed myself, slapped a band-aid over the black and blue goose egg on my forehead, turned my frown upside down and headed downstairs. The enticing aroma of fried bacon welcomed me before the girls did. I found them sitting around the table munching. Colt was bent over Amber, cutting a banana into her bowl of Rice Krispies. Bethany was reading a book while shoveling scrambled eggs into her mouth, and Callie ate a piece of toast while glued to the screen of her cell phone. A pretty typical morning in our house except I never fixed eggs and bacon on a school day. Colt would make some lucky woman a great wife one day.

"Hey there, Curly!" Having finished slicing the banana, he popped the last bit into his own mouth and threw the peel into my kitchen trash can. "Pull up a chair. The coffee is ready."

Amber patted the table. "Sit next to me, Mommy! Look what Colt made!"

Next to her bowl of cereal was a pancake as big as the plate it sat on – two banana slices for eyes, a mouth made of chocolate chips and whipped cream hair. "I can't eat it," she said solemnly. "It's too pretty."

Before my butt hit the chair, a steamy cup of brew was placed in front of me, already fixed to my liking – a teaspoon of sugar and a dash of cream. While I sipped, a plate of scrambled eggs, bacon and sliced tomatoes appeared. Holy cow. I wondered if I had I moved to Bizarre-o-world where mothers were treated as well as their children. "So, when did you guys get here?" I asked before scooping up some eggs.

"Your mom called the condo at six-thirty this morning," answered Colt. "She had somewhere to be. I told her I'd pick up the girls and bring them home for you."

I wanted to know why Howard didn't bring them, but was afraid of the answer, so I decided not to ask. At least not until the girls were gone.

"Man," I said smiling at my three beauties. "You must be tired."

"Not me." Amber was always in a good mood. The other two didn't look up or answer. They were probably pooped and grumpy.

"Mommy!" cried Amber, "tell us about the polar bear."

"Hmm?"

Bethany lifted her nose from the book. "Yes, Mom." Her voice carried a suspicious tone. "Tell us about the POLAR BEAR."

This must have been the story Colt concocted to explain last night's adventure. He could whip up a dandy breakfast, but I was beginning to worry about his skills with believable fiction.

He cleared his throat. "I told them to let you eat first, before you told them all about accidentally hitting the polar bear. You know – the one you hit with your van. Last night. And why they had to go to their grandmother's house."

"I got it Colt."

"Is he okay, Mommy? You didn't kill him did you?" Amber was very concerned.

"No—"

"I don't believe it," protested Bethany. There aren't any polar bears in Rustic Woods."

"Colt said it ex-scape-ted from the zoo."

"The only zoo around here is the Rustic Woods Zoo," she did finger quotes in the air when she said the word zoo, "and all they have there is a buffalo, a couple of goats, and an emu with a peg-leg."

Callie never looked up from her phone, but let us know how stupid she thought we all were by sighing loudly and mumbling, "Speaking of zoos . . ."

I didn't comment on Bethany's issue with the zoo, because it was true – the Rustic Woods Zoo was a poor excuse for an animal exhibit. The closest thing they had to a bear was a severely overweight opossum whose tail had been amputated after an unfortunate tangle with Snippy, the snapping turtle. "Well," I said, making the best of this sad excuse for an excuse, "he's fine, but they did have to medevac him to a polar bear hospital at the North Pole, because really, that's where they belong anyway. I mean, if a polar bear wanders around at night in Rustic Woods, he's only asking for trouble, right?"

"What's medevac?" asked Amber.

"It's an emergency helicopter," answered Bethany. Then she rolled her eyes. "I can't believe you're buying this story."

Amber stuck out her tongue at Bethany who had returned to better fiction than we were providing. "Mommy wouldn't lie to us, would you Mommy?" She touched my band-aid lightly. "Did you get hurt when you hit him?"

I nodded while wondering if I'd go to Hell for lying to my children. This was a little different than telling them that the green bits in the chicken and rice bake were chopped green apples instead of broccoli. Sometimes mothers just have to get the job done.

Callie jumped up from her chair and threw her backpack over one shoulder. "I'm outa here, freaks." She was gone before I could think of a reply.

I sipped my hot coffee. "She's in a mood today. I hope she doesn't fall asleep in school."

Colt was rinsing dishes in the sink. "She's been that way since I picked them up. She mumbled something about her father never being around and me being around too much and then she didn't open her mouth again."

"Yikes." It was hard enough raising a teen-ager, but adding a little marital strife into the mix made it even harder. "Okay girls," I said, changing the subject. "Go upstairs and get ready for school. You have to be at the bus stop in twenty minutes."

They cried out in unison, "Drive us, please! Drive us!" Their pleading eyes were too much to bear.

"But my van isn't here."

"Where is it?"

Actually, I didn't know where it was. I'd been left out of the loop.

"It's at the auto repair shop," Colt stepped in. "When you hit a polar bear, even if you don't hurt him very bad, it does a number on your bumper, trust me. I'll take you guys – I have to head out soon anyway. You can ride in The Judge and all of your friends will be jealous that you're being chauffeured in such a COOL car."

"It's an OLD car, with a silly name," sneered Amber as she and Bethany ran upstairs to brush their teeth.

"Did you hear that?" he asked, taking the seat next to mine. "No one appreciates a classic."

"It is a silly name."

He pretended to be shot in the heart. "Now that hurts."

"Is my van really at the auto repair shop?"

"Nope."

"Do you know where it is?"

He leaned in close and grinned. "I know everything, beautiful."

"Evidence?"

Colt nodded and sat back again. "What were you doing out so late anyway?"

I grinned back. "I thought you knew everything."

"I know you were out in the middle of the night and hit a woman who'd been shot three times by a 45 caliber pistol at close range. A Glock 21 – nice item. Wish I had me one."

"How do you know that?"

"Do you really need to ask?"

"Connections?"

"Every PI has them. Especially super sexy ones like myself. But those connections didn't tell me why you were out so late."

Shaking my head, I began my sorrowful tale. "This crackpot on Green Ashe Place named Bunny."

"Bunny Bergen – the one that Fredo mentioned?"

I shook my head. "His name is Waldo. And yes, Bunny Bergen – you know her?"

He smiled. "Not intimately."

"Stop it – how do you know her?"

"I don't really. She stopped by the condo one day looking for Howard. Said she was a friend of the family."

"How would she know where he lives?"

"You mean she's not a friend of the family?"

"A friend of the Addams Family maybe, but not mine. Howard's up to something . . ."

My face started that puckering thing it does before the tear ducts start to fill. I didn't want to cry. I tried really hard not to in fact. It was a sign of weakness and I had worked so hard the last few months to be strong. To be the heroine in my own life and in my daughters' eyes. Well, that wasn't going so well these days. Before I knew what was happening, the tears were spilling out onto my cheeks like lake waters overflowing the dike.

"Curly," Colt hugged me. "What's wrong?"

"I'm an idiot."

"You're a lot of things, but you're not an idiot."

"I am. I'm a boob and an idiot. He wasn't home this morning was he? That's why you brought the girls."

He nodded.

"It's all my fault. This date me and win me back thing was my idea and now single women are falling at his feet. How can I compete with a body like Bunny Bergen's? I'm losing him."

"Trust me – if there's one thing I know, you're not losing him. Quick – dry those eyes. I hear the girls."

I had just wiped my face clean when Bethany and Amber appeared with sweaters on and backpacks filled.

"Were you crying, Mommy?" asked Amber. "Is it the polar bear?"

"That's it. The polar bear. The polar bear hospital just called me on my cell phone and told me that he's just fine – he'll be fishing in cold waters any day now. These are happy tears."

Amber hugged me tight. "I love you."

I kissed her head of red curls. She smelled so good. "I love you too."

Bethany came in for a hug next and whispered in my ear. "Your cell phone is in the other room on the coffee table. It's been there since yesterday."

I'd been caught. "Thanks," I said when she pulled away. "I love you too honey. We'll talk about all of this. Soon."

She smiled. So did I, but it was a bittersweet smile. They grow up too fast.

Colt scooted the girls out the door and said he would check in later. I was nibbling the last of my eggs when the phone rang. Part of me didn't want to bother even looking to see who it was. I was tired, my body hurt and I just wanted to be left alone. The other part of me wondered whether the caller might be Howard. I succumbed, even though my muscles screamed at rising from the chair and taking two steps to the phone.

Despite my deep love for Peggy, I was disappointed to see her name on the caller ID. Okay, I'd answer and whine that Howard hadn't called me.

"Hi, Peg."

"You sound down in the dumps."

"If there's something lower than the dumps, that's where I'm at."

"Up for company? I've got a few minutes before I need to start errands."

"Sure. Colt made coffee and it's still warm."

I hadn't even placed the receiver back in its cradle when I heard a light tapping on my front door.

"Come in Roz!" I yelled.

The door opened. "How did you know it was me?" she asked as she came around into the kitchen from the foyer.

"You're the very essence of polite. Someone else would have rung the doorbell. You didn't want to bother me if I was resting."

"I try," she smiled. "The sky is looking really nasty out there. Are we supposed to get rain?"

"Haven't caught the news for days now. We could be expecting the latest snowstorm in recorded history and I wouldn't know it."

"How do you feel?"

I pulled a coffee mug from the cupboard and handed it to her while pointing to the coffee pot. "You know that scene in The Matrix when Neo practices jumping between buildings but he doesn't make it and falls to the ground, but it's not really the ground, and he wakes up in the real world again?"

She stirred cream into her coffee. "What's The Matrix?"

"Come on! I know you don't watch many movies, but EVERYONE knows The Matrix."

She shook her head. "Who's in it?"

"Never mind. The magic is lost now. I feel like crap. My whole body hurts. You would have thought that the tree branch came to life and beat me up after I hit my head on it."

We sat at the table. "Is Howard here?"

"Nope."

"Oh."

"I know. Don't ask me why his car is here and he isn't. There was no note, nothing. And it gets better. He wasn't home this morning when my mom called him to pick up the girls."

She cringed. "Sorry."

"I'll call him in a few minutes, when I feel like I can talk calmly instead of flipping out and going all Judge Judy on him."

"So no more news, then?"

"My van is being held for evidence. I wonder if I should use Howard's or get a rental?"

"Nothing about Michelle?"

We heard the door swoosh open followed by a, "Ciao, Bella!"

"Roz is here too!" I hollered. "Forgot to tell you – Peggy's coming over."

"Oh good!" Peggy said, making her kitchen appearance while fixing her wild red hair. "Mama Mia, has the wind started whipping up out there. It looks like the clouds are going to open up and dump buckets any minute." Her face lit up when she saw the half-full coffee pot. "Oh! May I?""

"Help yourself."

She snatched a mug from my cupboard and poured. "So, before I took the boys to school this morning, I stopped by the Alexanders' house to see if I could help in any way." She shook her head. "It's bad."

I was as anxious as Roz to hear how Michelle was doing. "What did her husband say?"

"I didn't talk to him."

"What's his name?" asked Roz.

Peggy sipped. "Lance. Lance Alexander."

"That's it," said Roz with a nod.

"Anyway, his sister was there," Peggy continued as she sat across from me. "She said Michelle was in intensive care in critical condition – a coma. They're not sure she'll live."

We listened sorrowfully. The reality sunk in and we had nothing else to say. A clap of thunder rattled the walls. Rain drops spattered against the window in front of my kitchen table. Leaves and bits of tree branches flew every which way. The sky was black even though it was only nine o'clock in the morning.

"Ouch," said Peggy. "Maybe my errands will have to wait."

"So," Roz asked, getting back to the Michelle story, "his sister is taking care of their kids while he's at the hospital?"

"Well, she's taking care of the kids, but she told me he was at the police station this morning."

Roz stood. "You still have those shortbread cookies?"

"Counter, next to the toaster."

She brought the box over. "Do you think he knew about the fight Michelle had with Bunny?"

"Bunny said something about Michelle and Lance being in counseling, remember that?" I nibbled on a cookie myself.

"If they're having marriage troubles, she may not be talking to him." Roz was dunking her cookies into her coffee.

"I wonder how bad their problems are." Peggy looked like she might take a shortbread herself, then shook her head and continued. "Killing bad, maybe?"

Roz furrowed her brows. "You think it was Lance?"

"Just wondering is all."

"I'm sticking with the Bunny theory. All signs point to Bunny with a gun, I'm sorry."

A powerful flash of light was followed by a house-jolting clap of thunder, causing us all to jump.

But it wasn't the thunder that made me drop my cookie and scream.

It was Bunny Bergen staring at us through my window, bathed in the lightning flash sopping wet and bug-eyed just like Sissy Spacek in *Carrie*.

Chapter 9

Roz ran outside, but returned a minute later soaked and Bunny-less. "I don't know how she could have disappeared that fast, but she did." She dried herself with one of my kitchen hand towels. "Two vans just pulled up in your driveway. They must have scared her away."

I met a man at the door. With a clipboard in his hand and scowl on his face, he informed me that "a Mr. Howard Marr" had called for a rental van. He didn't look overjoyed to be delivering in downpour. I smiled and signed four different pages, initialed at least ten times on three more pages, and accepted the keys and instructions from him in return.

"A sign of true love," I said returning to the table. "Now, if only my husband would make an appearance. To see how I'm doing maybe." I dropped into my chair. "Back to Bunny. She's gonzo up here." I tapped a finger to my head. "I say she's definitely homicidal."

Peggy nodded. "I agree she's a little pazzo."

"We need to tell someone what we saw at the school last night, and we need to tell them now."

Roz worked the towel through her blonde bob. "What do you suggest? You already told Howard."

"He said it's a police matter, so we go to the police."

Roz finished drying and handed me the towel. "I have to get up to the school and check the PTA in-box."

"And I have to get to the grocery store," said Peggy. "We're out of pasta."

"I have to go to the school too. Let's meet up afterwards. Where?"

"My house," offered Peggy.

"So we meet up at Peggy's house, then we'll call the police and be done with it. I'll feel better if I get this off my chest."

"Okay," agreed Roz. "I just hope we're doing the right thing."

"What could be the harm in it?" I asked rhetorically.

Weeks earlier I had signed on to volunteer in Bethany's class for a Spring Fling gardening project. Given the circumstances, I wasn't exactly in the Spring Fling mood, but I didn't want to be the mom that backed out of a commitment, so I fixed my hair a little and threw on some makeup. As usual, there wasn't an umbrella to be found in my house, so I had to step out uncovered.

As I locked my door to run out, already two minutes late for Spring Fling, Waldo appeared as if from thin air.

"Morning, Barbara." He smiled and I winced. The man really needed a cosmetic dentist.

"How do you do that?"

"What?"

"Sneak up on people. You're not there and suddenly you are there."

"I hope I didn't scare you again."

"Truthfully? It is a little creepy." I fumbled with the unfamiliar fob to unlock the rental van. "Don't take this the wrong way, but I'm late."

"Did you get a new car?"

"This is a rental while mine is at . . . the mechanic." I finally found the right button to unlock.

Luckily, he didn't seem too interested in my car problems. "I was just out for an invigorating morning walk," he said. "Get the blood flowing you know."

While the heavy torrents had slowed to a steady but light spring shower, it still didn't seem like an ideal day for a walk, invigorating or no. "Good. Have fun." I pulled on the door handle and climbed in, but I didn't get the door closed before he piped up.

"Did you hear about poor Shelly?"

Hmmm. I stopped. "Who's that?"

"Shelly Alexander. In the hospital."

"Yeah. I heard. Pretty awful." I pulled the door a little closer. "But I've never heard anyone call her Shelly before."

"No? My mistake. I thought she went by Shelly. Do you know what happened?"

"You don't?"

Waldo shook his head.

"Me neither." I closed the door, pulled my seat belt across, clicked and waved before starting the engine. Waldo returned the wave and moved aside while I backed out. Thankfully, I didn't hit a single mother on my drive from home to the school.

The rain had picked up again by the time I nosed into an empty space in the school parking lot. My luck was changing for the better. Finding open spaces in the lot during a school day is less likely than winning a hundred million dollar lottery on February 29th. I used my jacket for cover so I wouldn't be soaked by the time I reached the front doors. Halfway to the entrance, I met up with Shashi Kapoor. She had a golf umbrella and offered me half.

"I'm surprised to see you here today," she said as I stepped under.

"Why?"

"I have friends in high places – benefit of being a crossing guard. I heard about thees accident last night."

This was my worst fear. The Rustic Woods Rumor Mill was about to start churning at full speed. I felt sick to my stomach. "Ugh," was all I could muster.

"Do not worry. Your secret, it is safe with me. Mum is the word. Do not be surprised when you walk in today, though."

"What are they saying?"

"Most people know she is in hospital, very few people know how bad it is, and I do not think anyone knows why she is there."

"Do you know . . . everything?"

"That she was shot before you hit her?" She nodded.

"What are your friends in high places saying?"

"My friends are not talking about suspects, if thees is what you mean. I'll let you know if I hear more."

Well, I thought, they probably didn't have Bunny Bergen on their radar, but I'd make sure that changed real soon. We had reached the front door. A peek at my watch told me I was very late for the wet Spring Fling. "Thanks for sharing your umbrella and your information, Shashi."

"Like I said, the benefits of being a crossing guard." She turned around and headed to her cobalt Toyota sedan that had its own parking space right in front of the school. Another benefit of being a crossing guard.

Hoping to avoid human contact, I kept my eyes on the floor as I headed to the volunteer sign-in at the front office. I just wanted to get into Bethany's class, do my thing and get out. Breathing a sigh of relief when I found the receptionist chair empty, I scribbled my name quickly on the list and turned, ready for a quick get-away. Unfortunately, I ran right into Bunny Bergen's buoyant bosom.

She didn't look much better than when she shoved her spooky face in my window just two hours earlier. Her hair was still damp and pasted to her head and she wasn't suited up in her usual Model Mom attire. Instead, her worn blue sweatpants hung on the droopy side and the olive green Gap sweatshirt didn't even match. I was shocked. Who knew that Bunny owned a pair of sweatpants?

Our eyes met for only a second. I don't know if she was pretending that she didn't see me, or just embarrassed, but her gaze darted to the floor and she stepped around to the student sign-out log. She scribbled hurriedly then zipped back to the main hallway where teachers had escorted her two boys out to meet her. The trio was out of the building before I could say Holy Murderer-on-the-lamb Batman.

The Spring Fling had been postponed to a sunny day when planting would be a more enjoyable activity. The teacher asked me if I wouldn't mind making some copies for her. Was I going to say "No" to a teacher? Certainly not, but making copies was as high on my list of fun things to do as scooping runny dung from the kitty litter box.

But in the copier room I ran into Roz.

"Fancy meeting you here," I said. "Did you see Bunny?"

"No, did you?"

"Can you believe it? In the office."

"Did you talk to her?"

"She didn't seem interested in talking. Thank goodness. She signed her boys out early."

"Wonder what that's all about."

"She's probably fleeing the country as we speak."

"You're being a little dramatic." She changed the subject, most likely to keep me calm. "I tried to call Peggy a minute ago. She didn't pick up at home or on her cell."

"Maybe she was in line at the grocery store. I don't pick up my phone if I'm shopping."

"Maybe." She looked at her watch. "It's almost noon now. Should we just go over?"

I nodded. "When we're done. Good news by the way – Shashi Kapoor says she'll keep me up to date if she hears anything on the suspect front."

"How would she know?"

"She says she has friends in high places. I think it's that policeman who's always hitting on her when she's on crossing guard duty." The copier stopped. "I'm going to take these copies back to Bethany's teacher then head to Peggy's."

"I have to meet with the principal about this yearbook thing." She rolled her eyes. "I'll get there when I can."

When I returned the copies to the teacher, she sweetly asked if I could staple them and staple into handy study packets. Any classroom volunteer knows that sorting and stapling is even more boring than copying, but what's a good mother to do?

Two paper cuts and a stapling blister later, I stepped outside to dry sky. The drab gray clouds were breaking, and promising patches of azure shone through. When I pulled up to Peggy's house a few minutes later, her entire street was bathed in sunlight, and I finally felt like smiling again. Her van was in the driveway. The Rubenstein's house was a traditional brick front colonial, common in Rustic Woods, but it had a distinctly Peggy flavor. Most notably, the Italian tile plaque in her flower garden that welcomed guests - *Benvenuti amici!* I parked at the curb and crossed the lawn to the front stoop. I would have knocked on the glossy catsup-red door, but it was slightly ajar, so I pushed it open and hollered my usual, "Yoo hoo! Anybody home?"

No answer. I stepped in. We were good enough friends that I had no worries about entering her house without an invitation, but I didn't want to scare her since I hadn't called first. Roz had once and Peggy jumped her with a fireplace poker.

"Peggy? Are you here?" I walked through the living room to the family room. No sign of her. I yelled a little louder in case she was upstairs in her bedroom. "Peggy? It's Barb!" Silence. Not a footstep. I pulled out my cell phone and dialed hers. One ring in my ear was followed by a chirp from the kitchen. Another ring, another chirp from the kitchen. I followed the chirping and located Peggy's cell lying on her kitchen counter near the sink.

Ordinarily, I wouldn't have worried, but the strong odor of gas gave me pause. Nausea set in. I yelled her name one more time before covering my mouth and nose with my hand. As I turned to the stove, my gaze fell on the refrigerator. A message was scrawled on a magnetic white board. A message written in blood.

Three words.

Ease his pain.

Chapter 10

I think I ran out the door, but I'm not sure. I might have teleported. All I remember is standing on Peggy's front lawn talking to a 911 operator.

"I'm at 2121 Dogwood Blossom Court. My friend is missing and her house smells like gas," I sputtered.

"Are you in the house?"

"No."

"Is anyone else in the house?"

"No."

The lady operator was calm and efficient. "Why do you think your friend is missing?"

"There was a note."

"Where?" she asked.

"In the house."

"But you're not in the house, right?"

"No I'm not in the house, but I was in the house and now I'm not in the house and it smells like gas and Peggy isn't here and there's a note written in blood." I was definitely babbling.

"I understand you're upset," she said. "But I need you to stay calm."

"Why does this keep happening to me?"

She paused so long I thought I'd lost my connection. "This has happened before?"

"Not exactly. I mean no. Can you just send someone please?"

"I've already dispatched fire and police Ma'am. Would you like me to stay on the line until they arrive?"

"No." I disconnected without thinking. Then I dialed Roz. Voicemail.

"Roz. Come to Peggy's quick. Bad. It's very bad."

Disconnect. I dialed Howard. Voicemail. Damn!

I screamed to no one in particular. "Doesn't anyone answer their phones anymore?" That's when I noticed a gray and bent lady two houses down, sweeping her driveway and giving me queer looks. "Have you seen Peggy Rubenstein?" I shouted. The lady dropped her broom and ran into her house.

My head was pounding when the first police cruiser arrived followed by two fire trucks and three more cruisers. The street was alive with disaster. A police officer introduced himself and asked what the problem was.

"I came by to see my friend but she's not here and the house smells like gas and there's a note written in blood on the refrigerator. And I don't know if this matters, but I hit a woman with my van last night. She'd already been shot three times at close range. Maybe it's related. Maybe not."

That probably wasn't the best thing to say.

The officer cocked his head and took a silent beat. Finally he asked, "Are you Agent Marr's wife?"

"Do you know Howard?"

"No, but we've heard of you. I mean, him."

Just then a fireman loaded with equipment stepped up. Just my luck, it was stud muffin Russell Crow.

I cringed. "Me again."

He acknowledged me, but was all business. "Where's the problem?"

"She smelled gas in the house," said the officer. "You said your friend is missing. Did you go through the whole house?"

I shook my head.

"We'll check it out," said Crow. He was off to save the world. Or at least to find a gas leak.

A second uniformed policeman joined us while the first asked more questions. "Where is the bloody note again?"

"On the refrigerator. It said, 'Ease his pain'."

A few questions later, Russell Crow gave the all clear for the police to enter. "No leak. The gas oven was on without a flame."

My friendly cop told me to stay near the cruiser while they investigated. About that time I spotted a helicopter circling the neighborhood. Gawkers had started congregating on the sidewalks and in the street.

Suddenly someone was talking in my ear. "What's this all about?"

I jumped a mile high. It was Waldo. Again. "Dammit!" I screamed. "Now you're really starting to piss me off. You're like Huggermugger Houdini."

"Thank you."

"It's not a compliment."

"Is everything okay?"

"Waldo, I'm not in the mood . . ."

He put a clammy hand on my shoulder. "Barbara, I can see you are tense and at times like this, sometimes we just need our space. I'm going to grant you that space. But just remember, I'm always here if you need me. Always."

As he walked away, several policemen began putting up barriers – to keep out the riff raff, I guessed. Wish they had done that a few minutes earlier.

Seconds after the barriers were placed, Roz screeched up in her mini-van. No one was letting her past. I was about to beg the nearest police officer, but Colt appeared waving a badge and a smile and next thing I knew they were at my side.

I hugged Roz then turned to Colt. "How did you know I was here?"

"I stopped by your house and didn't find you there. When I heard the Fairfax County Police helicopters, I decided to follow them. Figured you'd be close to the trouble if not the cause of it."

I punched him in the arm. "I'm really scared. Peggy's door was open, she's not there, the oven was on without a flame and there's a note written in blood on her refrigerator."

Roz looked beside herself. "What did it say?"

"Ease his pain."

"Where have I heard that before?" asked Colt.

I would have answered, but a different policeman stepped up with a tube of red liquid in his hands. He held it up for us to see. "We're ninety-nine-point-nine percent sure your bloody note isn't really blood. It looks like this is the medium."

I asked the obvious question. "What's that?"

"Oh!" A shout came from behind us. "That's mine!"

We turned around to see Peggy standing on the other side of the barricade, smile pasted on her pale Irish-freckled face. "What's going on?"

"Is that your missing friend?" asked the cop.

If an artist had been around to render a caricature sketch of me, I would have looked like Elmer Fudd with a sunburn and steam coming out of my ears.

"Yes, sir," answered Roz. "That's our friend."

It didn't take long for the Fairfax County law enforcement and rescue services to pack up and head out. Russell Crow the handsome fire fighter stopped by to make sure I was okay. That was nice.

"I'm fine. Embarrassed, but fine," I said.

"Don't worry," he assured me. "We've seen crazier."

Colt felt he had to put his two cents worth in. "Just stick around this one. She raises the bar on the definition of crazy."

Inside the house, the two remaining police officers took down Peggy's official story. I'm not sure whether it was required for their report, or whether they just needed a good laugh.

Basically, it went like this – Peggy had decided to put a casserole in the oven for Michelle's family. She forgot, as she often does, that her pilot was on the fritz and that she had to light it by hand. She had her writing class on her mind, so she was a little distracted. Just before she stepped out to check in on an elderly, house-ridden neighbor, she was struck with moment of literary genius. An idea popped into her head, but she had to run out the door fast because she needed to get back before the casserole was done. She grabbed the nearest thing she could find, a vial of fake blood from her son's Halloween costume which had been lying in their kitchen all of these months. She dipped her finger in and wrote out the brilliant words, "Ease his pain," then ran out to her neighbor's. She figured she must have slammed the door, but it didn't catch. That's why it was open when I arrived.

The most amazing part of that story was that none of us knew that Peggy was taking a writing class.

"But Peggy," I said. "That line has already been used."

"Where?"

"*Field of Dreams.* You know, the movie with Kevin Costner. 'If you build it, he will come'?"

"I LOVE that movie." A look of horror crossed her face. "I'm a plagiarist."

"I don't think anyone will sue."

The two uniformed men scribbled a few more notes then left with grins on their faces. They probably figured that was the most fun they were going to have all day.

"Well, I have some interesting news," said Peggy after they left. "Just now, on my way back, I ran into the Alexander's neighbor. She said that Michelle is still in the ICU in critical condition. And Lance Alexander is being held for suspicion of attempted murder."

Chapter 11

"My, that's terrible news."

Everybody turned to see Waldo had joined our group.

This guy was like a bad virus that wouldn't die. "Waldo, I thought you were going for a walk."

"I have a route." He pointed up the street. "I turn around at Black Cherry Tree Lane. I'm on my way home now."

Lucky us.

"I have to say," he continued, "that I just can't imagine Lance Alexander doing such a thing. He loves her so deeply." He shook his head as if feeling Lance's pain. "Calls her his Pooh Bear."

"What did you say?"

"She told me that was his nickname for her. Pooh Bear. Why?"

"Nothing."

Colt's eye narrowed. He didn't care for Waldo. In fact I think he disliked him even more than I did. "Don't you need to keep moving to make a walk worth the effort?"

Waldo stared at Colt for a few silent seconds. "I'm detecting negative energy. I know some exercises to help relieve tension, or if that doesn't work, I could prescribe an excellent anti-anxiety medication."

Colt didn't respond, but I knew him. He was imagining a far more effective tension reliever – using Waldo as a punching bag.

I thought Colt's negative energy might have shut Waldo up, but it didn't. "Anyway, I heard that Bunny Bergen and Michelle had a fight after the PTA meeting last night and Bunny threatened to kill Michelle. In my mind, that makes Bunny far more suspect than Lance."

I looked at Roz and Roz looked at Peggy. Peggy was scraping at something on her shirt.

How did Waldo know about the fight? We were the only three around. Then I remembered the other car.

"Did you tell the police this story?" Roz was talking slowly and cautiously.

"Well," Waldo cleared his throat. "No. Technically, my words would be hearsay, since I didn't personally observe the argument. Probably not my place to approach the police."

I squinted at Waldo long and hard. What was he up to? I wondered if his "source" had mentioned that we were there when the Bunny and Michelle ruckus went down. If so, was he hinting that we should come forward?

Peggy must have finally been paying attention, because she piped up. "But, wait a minute—"

Roz cut her off at that pass. "Peggy, you need to get that casserole actually COOKING, don't you? Come on, I'll help." She moved Peggy toward her house and I could see there was some whispering going on.

Looking at my watch gave me a good reason to cut the conversation short. "Hey!" I yelled to them, "I have to get back to the house, Callie will be home any minute and I don't think she has her key."

Colt and I left faster than two convicts on a prison break, leaving Waldo all alone on the sidewalk.

Two minutes later we were in my house and I was standing in the front of the refrigerator trying to decide between a cold iced tea or a cold glass of wine. Colt grabbed an apple from my fruit bowl. Taking a milk carton from the top shelf, I abandoned the idea of tea or wine in lieu of good ol' fashioned Oreos and milk. The best way to drown my sorrows.

Colt munched while I savored the milk-soaked cookies. In between bites, I pried for information. "Howard's car is still out front. Have you seen him at all?"

He chewed, but didn't respond.

"Hello? Are you ignoring me?"

"Yes."

"Yes, you're ignoring me?"

"No, I'm not ignoring you. Yes, I've seen him. Barely in passing."

"Why wouldn't he at least come by for his car?"

"I have no idea. Can we talk about something else?"

"Why did you stop by?"

"Because you ran over a woman last night and I thought you might still be a little shaken up. Just checking in because I care. Should I leave?"

"No, no." I rubbed his arm. "I'm glad you're here and I'm glad you care." He played around with the apple, which was nearly all core now. I'd eaten five Oreos already and was trying to decide if I should really have another. "I need your advice."

"I feel very important. Ask away." He got up and threw the apple core into my trash can, then sat down and dug into the Oreos. I broke down and took another as well.

"We think Bunny Bergen shot Michelle Alexander."

He raised an eyebrow. "Who is "we" and why do "we" think this?"

"Roz, Peggy and I. We saw them fighting after the PTA meeting—"

"You mean that really happened?"

I nodded.

"How did Weldon—"

"Waldo."

"How did he hear about it?"

"Don't know."

"Did anyone else see it?"

"There was another car there that took off afterwards."

"Did you recognize the car? Any idea who was in it?"

"No. What are you thinking?"

"Just wondering. Go on."

"So anyway, Bunny accused Michelle of talking about her behind her back and said 'I'll kill you.'" I drew finger quotes for emphasis, "if she did it again."

Colt grabbed another Oreo, but didn't say anything for a minute. "Do you really think she'd kill someone? People say things like that without thinking."

I washed down the cookie with the last of my milk and took a minute to let it settle. "She's been acting funny. Not ha-ha funny, but tooty-fruity funny, and today she showed up here in the middle of the storm and the lightning flashed and her face looked like something from a slasher movie and then she took her two boys out of school early."

"You're starting to sound like your friend Peggy."

The front door swooshed open and the house reverberated with the sounds of Callie entering the premises. That is to say the classic thumping of her backpack hitting the foyer floor and the ever popular slamming of the door so hard that the walls shook. Beautiful she was; graceful she was not. "Mom! I'm home." By the sound of her voice, she was in a good mood. When she came into the kitchen and saw Colt sitting with me, her mood and her feet made a u-turn. She walked out without a word.

"Callie, do you want a snack, sweetie? We have Oreos!"

"Not hungry," was her answer from the stairs. I counted. Five, four, three, two, one, SLAM! Her bedroom door. She had that timing down to an art.

With Callie home, I knew I had twenty minutes before I needed to be at the bus stop for Bethany and Amber. "So, to make a long story short, we think we should call the police and tell them what we saw. What do you think?"

"Sure. Absolutely."

"Really?"

"Any information is good information," he drummed the table. "So, what do you know about this Wadsworth guy?"

"Waldo."

"Yeah, but that's not his real name. What did he say it was again?"

"Why?"

"Just curious."

"Oswald Fuchs."

"I just took your last cookie." His grin was wily. "I like your cookies."

Taking my glass to the counter and throwing the empty Oreo package into the trash, I chastised him. "You are a piece of work, aren't you?"

"I'm a piece of art." He brushed crumbs from his hands. "Can I borrow your computer for a few minutes?"

"Yeah, it takes a few minutes to boot up though – we need a new one badly."

He was off in a shot to my small computer room around the corner. Technically it was a closet, but we wired it for light and electricity, and it served me just fine while I posted movie reviews and articles on my website. Meanwhile, I brushed my teeth, checked out the circles under my eyes, plucked a couple of hairs from my chin, and ran to the bus stop where I tried Howard again on my cell phone while I waited for the girls. I still couldn't reach him, but I did make a mental list of the things I had to do – laundry, dishes, pay a few bills, cook dinner, call friends and figure out a time to contact the police and report a potential killer.

Two hours after Amber and Bethany arrived home, the house was eerily quiet. Callie was still in her room, hopefully doing homework, but probably chatting online. Bethany was in her room definitely doing homework, Amber was on the living room couch watching the Disney Channel, and Colt was still in my computer room. I heard him talking on his cell phone a couple of times, but had no idea what he was doing. PI work I guessed, which was probably nothing more exciting than tracking down some guy who had written a few bad checks. I had scratched three of my to-do items off the list, but hadn't thought about food at all. I would hold off calling Peggy and Roz until after the dinner and bedtime rush.

Popping my head into the computer room, I found Colt grabbing a sheet of paper from my printer, folding it in half and stuffing it into his back jeans pocket. My gaze rested longer on his nicely shaped rumpus longer than it should have. I gave myself a mental slap. "Hey, I think I'm going to order in Chinese. You wanna stay and join us?"

"Can't thanks. Meeting some friends for dinner."

"You have friends?"

"I'm a very likeable fellow, you know." He tapped my nose playfully with his finger. "And I saw you staring at my cute butt."

I blushed, but ignored the comment. "Fine. I guess we'll eat alone. All the men in my life are leaving me."

"I'll never leave you, you know that." He took me in for a big hug which I savored long and hard.

"I love you—" I was about to finish that sentence with "you big lug," when he pushed me away like I had killer cooties.

I stared at him, momentarily confused.

He was looking past my shoulder. "Sorry, dude."

My heart dropped like an anchor as it splashed into a sea of dread. I turned my head, following Colt's gaze until my sights fell on Howard standing in the doorway. His jaw was set, his lips pressed thin. It was his hold-back-the-anger look. He closed the door behind him without ever taking his eyes off mine. He had caught us in an innocent act that didn't look so innocent. And to make matters worse, Callie was standing next to him and Amber had viewed the entire show from her prime position on the living room couch.

"Just great," shouted Callie. "I come downstairs to see if maybe you're going to feed us dinner sometime this century, and here you are playing kissy-face with your boyfriend. In front of Dad! Isn't life peachy in the Marr household? College can't come soon enough!" She flipped herself around and stomped back upstairs.

"Hi, Daddy!" Amber cheered.

Howard broke his somber stare-grip on me, turned to Amber with a beaming smile, and scooped her up in his arms. "Hi, Sweetie. How are you?"

"Good, Daddy. Can I show you my art project?"

"Absolutely, gorgeous. Let me go talk to Callie first, though, okay?"

Colt had been inching his way past Howard, trying to sneak out, but he wasn't successful.

"Did I scare you away?" asked Howard as Amber wriggled down out of his arms.

"You? No, no. I have friends. To meet. For dinner." He opened the door and was about to step out, but turned to me, "Meet you tomorrow at one, remember? Straight Shooters Gun Shop – you know where it is?"

I nodded. I actually had no idea where it was, but my vocal cords had frozen.

"Just teaching your wife to shoot a handgun, man. You okay with that?"

Howard didn't answer.

"It was her idea. Just so you know."

Howard shoved Colt out the door, closed it hard, then took a deep breath and made his way up the stairs, never once looking me in the eye.

"Mommy," Amber whispered, as if Howard might hear her. "Colt isn't your boyfriend, is he?"

"No, Amber. He's just my friend who happens to be a boy – well, a man. But he's not my boyfriend. And he's your father's friend too, so don't worry."

"I don't know," said Amber shaking her head, apparently not convinced. "I think Daddy just pretends to like Colt. If you axe me, he's jealous. Maybe 'cuz you hug Colt a lot." She proceeded back to the couch, where she flopped down and fixed her eyes on Disney again. "Can you fix supper now? I'm hungry."

"I'm ordering Chinese, is that okay?"

"Can you order those squishy noodles?"

She meant chicken lo mein. "Sure."

I heard Howard talking to Bethany, and then his footsteps moved to Callie's room. There was a light knock, and he must have been invited in because the door squeaked open then closed again. I felt so guilty I could have melted right into the floor. I decided it was better to just get things moving rather than pace a hole in the foyer floor, wondering when he'd come back down. I grabbed the phone and dialed Hunan Rustic Woods. The fact that I knew the number by heart probably didn't reflect well on my recent homemaking efforts. Well, I reasoned, it was healthier than Kentucky Fried, right? Anyway, the lady who took my order said it was a busy night – would be forty-five minutes before they could deliver. Fine, I'd cut up some apples to hold everyone over.

Finally I heard Howard's footsteps and the next thing I knew he was in the living room and Amber was talking his ear off then running for her art project. It was quite the project – I was very proud. I poked my head into the living room while she was out collecting her prize. He stood next to our tall wing-back chair, hand on hip, looking very confident and handsome in his black FBI jacket.

I took a few tentative steps toward him and risked an invite. "We're having Chinese, can you stay?"

Surprisingly, he reached out and pulled me in for a long, wonderfully warm, soft kiss. Holy cow. I wasn't about to fight it this time. I wrapped myself around him and joined in the fun. I think I heard birds singing.

Okay, the birds were probably my imagination, but the giggling I heard from upstairs was not. When we finished, I was smiling like a Cheshire cat and Amber was running up with her art project.

"See my project, Daddy? Those are two kitty cats, and that's a pond." She put his hand on the poster board. "Feel that? It's called texture. We're learning all about it in art. Do you like it?"

Howard was smiling, but still had his other hand resting nicely on my booty. "Yes, I love it. You did a beautiful job."

"I did, didn't I? Okay, I'll go away now, so if you want to go on smooching you can." Not bothering to see if we'd continue, she took off in a flash back up the stairs. Howard wrapped his arms around me again, and we stood, faces close, smiling.

"I tried to call you a couple of times," I said when she was gone.

"I know. I've been busy. Can't talk about it. Karl dropped me off here so I could get my car, but I have to go. Don't be mad."

"It's not another woman?"

"It's WORK. And you know I can't talk about it." His expression changed the way it does when he wants to change the subject. "Have you heard any news on the woman last night . . . what was her name?"

"Michelle Alexander. Peggy said she's still in intensive care."

I lowered my voice so Amber couldn't hear. "That's what I wanted to talk to you about—"

Howard followed my lead and whispered as well. "How well did you know her?"

"Not very. But I wanted to talk to you about—"

"You said she was at the PTA meeting about some yearbook problem?"

"Yes, she was, but would you stop interrupting me!" I pulled away. "I want to talk about Bunny."

"Barb. Leave it alone."

"But—"

He stopped me quietly, but firmly. "Leave it alone. Do you hear me? But we have to talk. I'll call you as soon as I can, okay?"

"You can't stay just for dinner?"

He kissed me again. Just as long, just as soft. "I wish I could."

I nodded. "Okay."

One more quick peck and he was out the door, but not before he repeated his warning. "Remember – leave it alone. Right?"

Knowing there were at least a few minutes until the food arrived, I decided to see if I could patch things up with Callie. I knocked on her door.

"Come in."

I turned the knob, pleased that it wasn't locked. She was sitting on her bed, propped up with pillows, reading a book.

"Whatcha reading?" I asked bouncy and fun, hoping she'd play along. She didn't. She gave me a cursory grimace and went back to her book. I peeked at the cover. "Romeo and Juliet. My favorite Shakespeare play."

"It's stupid."

Aha. Progress. At least she was responding. She wasn't looking at me, but words were exchanged. I was relieved that she didn't direct me to jump off a bridge or visit the home of eternal damnation.

"You should watch the movie version with Leonardo DiCaprio. Three minutes in and you're ready to stab them yourselves."

That got me a sneer, but no conversation. So much for progress.

I kept trying. "Has the wireless internet been working okay for you up here?" Callie's recent birthday present was her own laptop computer, but we had been having some trouble with the wireless router.

"Yup."

"Well, that's good right?"

She snapped the book closed so fast that I jumped. "I have to start a history paper now. Could you leave, please?"

I really didn't want to leave. I wanted to patch things up. But she was punishing me, which was understandable. After a brief pause, I decided to let her punish away. I would wait for the right time to make things better between us. "Sure," I said. "I'll call you down when dinner is ready."

"What are we having?"

"I ordered Chinese."

She grunted, which I had learned is teen-age speak for "It figures – you're such a loser."

I was about ready to close the door behind me when she said something faintly, but with biting sarcasm. "Thanks for asking, by the way."

"Asking what?"

"My point exactly. Close the door please."

Oh boy. Had I read her signals wrong? Should I have stayed and pressed for more information? Was I about to join Joan Crawford in the League of Despicable Mothers?

"Callie—"

"Close the door."

Reluctantly, I did as she said, but stood outside of her room wondering what I had or hadn't done. I briefly considered going back in to confront the issue head on, but thought better of it. It would probably only make things worse.

As I headed back down the hall to go downstairs, Bethany called from her own room. "It's Brandon."

She sat at her desk, glasses on her pretty little face, pen in hand looking very much the smart, hard worker that she was. This one would run the country some day, I was convinced. First female president.

"What about Brandon?" I asked as I stood outside her door. But as soon as the words were out of my mouth, I slapped my forehead and groaned. "Oh no!" I lowered my voice. "Did he ask her out?"

"I think so. She was talking to Daddy about it. I couldn't hear everything because the door was closed, but she was giggling."

Callie? Giggling? He must have asked her out. I took a deep breath and lamented my selfish stupidity. Not only was I the worst mother in the world, but I had also missed out on a very important maternal experience. This just wouldn't do.

"Thanks, Sweetie," I said. "Is your homework almost done?"

She nodded.

"Okay, well dinner should be here soon. I love you."

"I love you too, Mom."

Skulking downstairs, I tried to get a grip on the events unfolding. I was obsessing and my family was suffering the consequence. So what if Bunny was crazy? Did she try to kill Michelle Alexander? Not my problem. I was a mother first. Time to forget about the whole ordeal and take care of my own life and my own family. The police could find the shooter themselves. It was their job, after all, not mine. And Howard did tell me to leave it alone. I decided to listen to him. This time at least.

I kept money in a coffee can on our kitchen counter for emergency order-out meals. I was pulling out a twenty when I heard a tapping at my back door. No one ever tapped at my back sliding glass door. People always used our front or side door. This was more than odd. Goose pimples sprouted on my forearms.

Cautiously, I peeked around the cupboard to catch a glimpse – hoping it was friend, not foe. I wasn't pleased.

Not a bit.

My visitor was Bunny Bergen.

Chapter 12

Unfortunately, there is no clear etiquette for handling a wigged-out psycho killer who stops by for a visit. Especially when she's a mother in your neighborhood who seems to be preoccupied with ruining your life. I'd pulled my head back behind the cupboard, but it was silly to hope that she hadn't seen me. If I had seen her, reason would dictate that she had seen me too. She knew I was home.

Damn!

While I contemplated escape options, Bunny tapped again – louder this time. I was tempted to ignore her altogether and hope she just went away. This would be rude, but then again, so was plugging another mother full of bullets, so we would be even.

Tap, tap, tap.

Man, she wasn't giving up.

"Mommy, what's that noise?" Amber had wandered in and walked right past me before I could stop her. "Oh! It's Mrs. Bergen!" She'd blown my cover and I couldn't move fast enough to stop her. "Mommy, why aren't you letting Mrs. Bergen in?" She opened the sliding glass door.

That's what I get for teaching my kids good manners.

"I'm sorry, Bunny, I didn't hear you. Come in." I pushed the door open farther as if I really wanted her to enter my home. "Amber, Sweetie, would you go upstairs and, um, take a bath?"

"But isn't dinner going to be here soon?"

"Yes, but you really need a bath and it's getting late. Go upstairs."

"But—"

"Amber, NOW!" My shout was fast and sharp. Poor Amber looked hurt and a little scared. I felt terrible, but I needed her out of the way.

Bunny stepped inside and closed the door behind her. A paisley purse was slung over one shoulder and she clutched a small, brown suitcase. I would have been more worried if she didn't look so pathetic standing there all droopy-eyed like a lost basset hound.

"I'm sorry, Amber, I didn't mean to yell. Tell you what – just go up to your room and . . . get all of your things ready for bath time, that way it will go faster. Do that now for me, okay? No arguments."

"Okay," she said, walking away and giving me a suspicious look.

Bunny hugged her suitcase tighter. "Barb, I didn't know where to go or what to do. I'm afraid."

"Why are you afraid?"

"It wasn't me."

Uh oh. "What do you mean?"

"Michelle – I didn't try to kill her. Someone shot her before I got there."

Double uh oh.

"Mom!" Callie's voice screamed from upstairs. "Is the Chinese here yet?"

"Hang on!" I yelled back.

I felt like Michael Corleone in The Godfather III. *Just when I thought I was out . . . they pull me back in.* Not my favorite of the Godfather movies, but I understood the sentiment.

The synapses in my brain fired like a shock and awe campaign as I worked to resolve this newest predicament. Either I had a killer in my house or someone who had possibly witnessed an attempted killing. Regardless, the police had to be called. But first my kids needed to be fed and most importantly, kept safe. I decided to stow Bunny away until I could deal with her better.

"Bunny, follow me." I was calm on the outside but quivering on the inside. "Let's get you to a warm, safe place and we'll talk in a few minutes, okay? I have a guest room where you can rest, is that okay?"

She nodded and I saw tears well up in her eyes. "You're so nice, Barb."

Man, I wish she hadn't said that. I was about to send her to the Big House.

Up the stairs we went, Bunny clutching her suitcase like a toddler clutches a comfort blankie. I opened the guest room door and moved aside so she could go in. She spent a few seconds looking all lost-puppy again, staring around the room rather aimlessly, then she sat on the bed. She never let go of the suitcase.

"I'll be back up in a couple of minutes. I have to feed the kids." I used Roz's comforting tones from the day before. It seemed to be working. Probably that whole more-bees-with-honey theory. "You'll stay in here, right?"

She nodded again.

I closed the door, wishing I could lock her in there.

Then I made rounds to the girls' rooms telling them to get their tooshies downstairs for dinner. There were some groans when they heard Hunan Rustic Woods hadn't made the delivery yet, but they did what I asked, once I'd pointed out that they'd get the food faster if they were sitting at the table when it arrived.

We were all trampling down the stairs when the doorbell rang.

Hallelujah!

Callie opened the door and we were all relieved to see Mr. Chang, our favorite delivery man. He also owned Hunan Rustic Woods and evidently liked us so much that he sometimes delivered our orders personally. I ran for the money, and handed it over. "Thank you, Mr. Chang – you're a life saver!"

"Any time, Missus Ma," he said with a smile and a bow.

Bethany was already busy putting dishes and silverware out on the table while Amber and Callie opened the food cartons.

I had handled the hungry family. The police were next. I picked up the kitchen phone, but hesitated before dialing. Bunny's claim that she'd found Michelle already shot echoed in my memory. What if she was telling the truth? She had to come for me for help.

On the other hand, I reasoned, even if she was innocent, I should call the police and let them deal with it. Let her tell them her story, right? I clicked the 'talk' button on my phone. The phone beeped back at me. Of course, the beep-back meant my phone wasn't charged. We were always leaving it off the charging cradle.

"Mommy," asked Amber with a mouth full of lo mein, "aren't you going to eat?"

"Yes, honey," I said, looking around for my cell phone. "I will in a minute." I lifted a pile of school papers from the counter and peeked underneath. No cell. "I need to do something first."

"You should take some up for Mrs. Bergen – she might be hungry, too."

Again with the manners. I wanted to make that darn phone call and be done with it, but taking food to Bunny gave me a good reason to check on her. Who knew what she might be doing up there in my guest room?

"You're right. She might be hungry. Good idea." I rubbed her beautiful head of curls and scooped a few forkfuls of lo mein into a bowl, grabbed a fork, and ran upstairs. Halfway up, I remembered that my cell phone was in my jacket pocket. I had put it there after the fiasco at Peggy's.

Putting on my I'm-not-afraid-you're-a-killer smile, I opened the guest room door ready to hand Bunny her bowl of Chinese and pretend everything was just peachy keen, but stopped cold in my tracks when I saw her suitcase lying opened on the bed.

Actually, it wasn't the suitcase that stopped me cold. It was the bloody gun inside.

Chapter 13

Now the thing about wanting to learn how to shoot a gun is that a certain amount of preparatory research is advisable. Colt had suggested it. And I had listened. That's why I knew that the gun in Bunny Bergen's suitcase was a Glock 21 – the same model that had been used on Michelle Alexander.

If ever there was a time for jumping to conclusions, it was now.

The bowl of lo mein slipped from my hands and fell to the floor, crashing loudly and shattering into several pieces.

"Are you okay, Mom?" Bethany shouted.

"Fine! Just a little accident!" I answered. "Stay downstairs!"

I slammed the door shut and flipped the lock while Bunny dove to her knees and scooped up lo mein noodles. "I found it. It's not mine, I swear, Barb."

"Where?" My heart was thumping out of control and I started to feel a little dizzy. "Is this the one?"

"It was there when I found her." Bunny stood up. Lo mein noodles dangled from her hands. "But I wasn't thinking and I picked it up after. Now it has my fingerprints all over it – and Michelle's blood." Tears dripped onto the noodles. She attempted to dry her eyes with her shoulder. She couldn't have looked more pitiful if she tried. And I was actually starting to feel sorry for her.

Grabbing several tissues from the box on the dresser behind me, I told her to drop the lo mein noodles and clean her hands. We'd worry about the food mess later. We evidently had a much bigger mess to contend with.

She wiped her hands, dabbed her eyes with some fresh tissues, and sat down on the bed to compose herself.

"I'll be honest with you, Bunny," I said, trying to maintain composure. "You've been acting . . . a little more than strange lately. Then we saw you arguing with Michelle last night and you did threaten to kill her. But now you've brought this gun into my house and I'm REALLY not happy about that. I have my daughters to think about. So I'm giving you two minutes to explain yourself, and then we need to figure out how to get that gun out of here. Depending what you tell me, I may call the police to do it for me."

Despite my threat to call the police, Bunny had calmed down considerably. She nodded, then started her story. "I don't know what got into me after the PTA meeting." She sniffed and dabbed her eyes some more. "I was mad, but I didn't think I was *that* mad. But when I was talking to Michelle, my whole head felt like it exploded and I had this powerful urge to just scream at her. I even wanted to punch her. I don't know where it came from. I've never been a violent person ever. You know me. I'm a nice person."

I nodded, but I don't know why. I didn't know her well enough to agree or disagree.

"And those awful things just spilled out. So when I got home later, I felt just terrible. Then Michelle called me and said she really needed to talk and was I still mad? I apologized and told her no I wasn't still mad, and yes, let's talk. She told me to meet her at Cappuccino Corner. I was almost there when she called me on my cell and said 'they' were following her, she was sure of it. She had gone back home and snuck out the back door headed to the little playground in the woods. Did I have a flashlight and could I meet her there?"

"Who's 'they'?"

"I don't know! I had no idea what she was talking about. I was really confused, but she sounded terrified, so I just said I'd come."

Moms knew about the little playground in the woods. Many of the paths in Rustic Woods led to the delightful park that sat nestled among the trees. It sat next to a stream so kids could swing or slide or look for tadpoles in the water. But it was so deep in the woods that it would be impossible to find at night without illumination.

"Did you have a flashlight?" I asked.

She nodded. "A tiny one I keep on my purse so I can find my keys in the dark. It didn't help much, but I was able to make my way to the playground." Her face scrunched all up and she started crying again. "But not in time." She wept for a good minute before she was calm enough to continue. I was getting worried that the girls would hear her and come to see what was wrong.

"The first shot made me scream. It was just so loud. I've never heard anything like it, and then the other two came right after." She shuddered.

I handed over more tissues. "How far away were you?"

"Not far. I ran about, I don't know, one hundred feet? Two hundred?" She shook her head. "I'm not good with distances. And there she was on the ground by the slide. She wasn't making any noise and I was sure she was dead, but I got on the ground and shook her just to see. That's when she started moaning. I was so relieved. But it didn't last long. I thought she was dead. I'd run out of my house so fast that I forgot my cell phone, so I got up to run and find a house to tell someone to call 911. That's when I tripped on something. And I picked it up." She shook her head.

"The gun?" I asked.

She nodded. "I dropped it, but then realized it had my prints on it, so I picked it up again. I ran with it to my car, terrified that someone would see me with it and think I had killed her. So I drove home and that's when I called you."

I was stupefied. If Bunny was telling the truth, Michelle was a living miracle. She must have regained consciousness and, practically on death's doorstep, managed to walk out of the woods on the path that empties onto Tall Birch where I hit her while driving to Bunny's house. I couldn't have written a better, more exciting movie script if I'd tried. But I needed to figure out if Bunny was on the up and up. She did have the gun after all. She could have been fabricating the mysterious "they" story just to throw me off.

"Did she manage to say anything before you ran for help?"

"Yes," Bunny answered, her face blotched from all of her crying. "She said, 'In the Pooh Bear'."

"Pooh Bear?" Bunny couldn't possibly know that Michelle uttered those same words to me as well. "That's what she said to me!" I felt ready to jump out of my skin.

Bunny looked confused. "When did she talk to you?"

"Last night. I hit her when I was driving to your house. You didn't know?"

"No!" Her face lit up with understanding. "So that's what happened. So she wasn't found on the playground?"

I shook my head and stared her down. Her story made sense, and I was inclined to believe her. Of course, I'm one of these gullible saps that takes anyone at face value.

"She was still conscious after I hit her," I explained. "All she could whisper was 'Pooh Bear.' I heard today that's what her husband calls her, so I assumed she was talking about him. He's being held by the police. They think he did this. Do you?"

She blew her nose. "I don't know. He doesn't seem the type. Maybe though. But I'm pretty sure I know what she meant. I think she left a clue."

Chapter 14

It turned out that Bunny had a plan: find the clue.

The plan didn't involve calling the police first, and while I understood her position, I argued with her anyway. Tell the police where this clue was, I said. Let them figure it out from there. She wanted to find it herself then approach the police after. She thought having proof of her innocence would protect her. I wasn't so sure we'd find proof of her evidence, but by agreeing to help her, I got both Bunny and the gun out of my house, and I liked that part.

In retrospect, agreement may not have been a sane option, but at the time, I had no idea that some very sinister wheels were already in motion. Basically, I was damned if I did, damned if I didn't, so sane option or not, Hell was waiting for me right around the corner.

I didn't want to leave the girls alone in the house. Howard was working (so he said) and Colt was out with friends. This left me no alternative but to call my mother and ask her to take them. I needed a good lie though. The truth just wasn't an option. I happened to notice the stack of newspapers Bethany was collecting for donation to the Homeless Dog Rescue League. An obituary page crowned the pile. A lie was born. And a darned believable one if I do say so myself.

"Mom?" I said when she answered her phone. "Can the girls come to your place tonight?"

"Why on earth for? What's going on? Are you and Howard fighting?"

"No, Mom. A friend's favorite uncle just died unexpectedly. She asked me to take her to Baltimore to be with her mother. She's too upset to drive."

"That's so sad. Well maybe I should drive her. Then you wouldn't have to take the girls out. It's a school night after all."

"That won't work."

"Why?"

She would have to ask, wouldn't she? I hadn't thought the lie that far ahead. "Bunny's, afraid of people," I blurted out.

"What?"

"My friend, Bunny. She's very shy and nervous around people she doesn't know."

"Well, I'm a very amicable person—"

"Thanks, Mom!" CLICK.

Bunny closed up her suitcase and I loaded the girls into the rental van. I told them the same lie and they had no reason to doubt me since Bunny's face was still red and blotchy from crying. She sat up front, but we put the suitcase way in the back and I covered it with a pile of blankets from the house. I wanted to be as far away from that gun as possible. I don't know why I thought the blankets would help, but then again, I don't know why I thought following Bunny's plan would help either.

Just before leaving the house, I called Roz, and told her that I had Bunny with me, that I wasn't calling the police just yet, and that I'd be in touch with her as soon as I had more news. She said she thought I was crazy and I said maybe Bunny was rubbing off on me. She didn't laugh.

It was 7:05 when we pulled away from my mother's condo parking lot and the purple sky was darkening by the minute. I turned on my headlights. By 7:20, when we pulled in front of the Alexanders' house, it was officially night time. A car was parked in the driveway and we saw lights on through the windows of the classic, Rustic Woods contemporary style home. We assumed someone was home. Most likely, from what we'd been told, Lance's sister and Michelle's kids.

"Are you ready?" I asked Bunny, who had grown jittery during the drive across town.

"Yes," she said, tying her black rain coat a little tighter and taking a deep breath. "Ready."

Once on the front stoop, I pushed the doorbell. I couldn't hear if it rang or not. I always hate that, when you can't hear the bell. You wonder, should I ring it again? Is it broken? Should I knock? Of course, you don't want to annoy people, so you just stand there and wait, not really sure if anyone knows you're at the door or not. It's a precarious position to be in. Even more precarious when you intend to burglarize the home you're hoping to enter.

A long, thin window that flanked the left side of the door enabled me to look inside and see a person coming our way. A moment later the door opened and a small, demure looking woman appeared. By her looks I would have said she was in her mid forties. Her dark, straight hair was pulled back in a pony-tail and she wore plastic frame glasses on a thin and somewhat pointy face. She didn't say anything, just gave us a hesitant, questioning look as if that was sufficient for us to start explaining our visit.

"Hi," I said, extending my hand for a shake. "My name is Barbara Marr. This is Bunny Bergen. We know Michelle, and we just wanted to stop by, offer our condolences to Lance and see if there was anything we could do to help. Is Lance here?"

"No, I'm sorry he's not. I'm his sister, Julia." Her handshake was firmer than I'd expected for how low-key she seemed. "Would you like to come in?"

That's what we were hoping for. "Maybe just for a minute." Once inside, she led us back a few steps to a small living room where Bunny and I sat on a couch and Julia sat in a small Queen Anne chair.

"How is she doing?" Bunny asked.

Julia sighed. "It's touch and go, truthfully," she said, just above a whisper. "Michelle's parents are at the hospital right now, and her brother just took the kids out for supper. They needed some sort of distraction. Poor things."

I wondered why she was whispering if the kids weren't in the house. Probably just her way. It did make me worry that someone else might be around though. The fewer people the better for Bunny's plan to be a success.

Obviously distraught, Bunny grabbed a tissue from her coat pocket. "Do you mind if I use the restroom?" she asked.

"Of course, it's—"

Bunny was already on her feet. "I know where it is. Thank you." She was gone in a flash.

"Are you close friends with Michelle?" asked Julia when we were alone.

"Bunny and Michelle were . . ." I jumped when Bunny slammed the bathroom door very loudly. I cringed apologetically, then continued. "They were quite close. I really only knew her as an acquaintance." I shook my head, mortified when I realized that I had just referred to Michelle in the past tense. "I'm so sorry! I mean they ARE close and I KNOW her as an acquaintance. Positive thoughts, right? I'm sure she'll pull through." I was glad I didn't slip and say I was the one who had nearly done her in myself by running her over in the dead of the night or that the gun used to shoot her was in the back of my rental van. Some things are better left unsaid.

"We're all praying," said Julia with as much smile as she could muster.

I was worried about what Bunny was up to down the hall, so small talk wasn't exactly on the tip of my tongue. Awkward silence filled the air. Luckily or not so luckily, Bunny came to the rescue by wailing very loudly from the bathroom.

Julia sat up straight and furrowed her brow. "Is she okay?"

"Well, she was very upset when she heard about Michelle. And she's been . . . out of sorts anyway. She probably just needs some time." I was beginning to regret sending Bunny in on this job. She didn't exactly have all of her wits about her to pull off a James Bond-like maneuver.

"I hope she doesn't wake MoMo. He's been very cranky lately."

Uh oh.

"MoMo?" I asked, panic setting in.

"My son, Morgan. We call him MoMo. He's been a grumpy Grumperson all day and finally fell asleep on Michelle and Lance's bed."

Holy cow. The plan was for Bunny to get the Pooh Bear from the dresser in their bedroom. If MoMo the brat had set up camp in there we were in deep doo doo. Bunny quieted down, so I pressed on, trying to keep the charade going even though I really just wanted to run out the door and call the police to come gather the clue themselves.

"She sounds like she's calm now. I'm so sorry." I cleared my throat. "How is Lance taking all of this?"

Suddenly, Julia became very animated. "Oh! It's just awful," she said, her hands going into the air in a gesture of disbelief. "His wife is in the hospital fighting for her dear life and he can't even be with her!"

"Why is that?"

"The police are holding him for questioning as a suspect, can you believe it?"

Two loud thumps turned Julia's attention toward the hall. Worried that Bunny was bungling our mission, I scrambled to keep Julia talking. "Really?" I said. "That's awful. Tell me more."

"He has a lawyer, but there's been no bail posted, and the police won't discuss the matter with anyone in the family. Even the lawyer won't tell us anything. Our father is at the police station right now trying to get some answers." She was shaking her head and pursing her lips. "This whole thing is a nightmare like I've never seen."

"Wow." The comment was lame, I know. My conversation-machine was on the fritz.

Bunny returned and sat back down stiffly on the couch next to me. "I'm sorry," she said to Julia. "I'm not feeling well. Could I have a glass of water?"

"Oh. Um, sure." Julia didn't seem keen on hostessing, but she stood, if somewhat grudgingly, and disappeared into the kitchen.

"There's a kid in the bedroom," Bunny whispered.

"MoMo – her son."

"MoMo? What kind of name is that?"

That sure was the crackpot calling the kettle black. "Why were you making that awful noise?"

"I was trying to wake him up so he'd leave."

If I were a hitting woman, I would have slapped her silly. "That's a stupid idea. And it didn't work. Although I'm sure you woke a few corpses."

"I know. I'm not thinking clearly."

"Why didn't you just sneak in? Kids sleep through anything."

"I tried that too."

I didn't like the sound of that. "Tried?"

"It's not there."

I heard glasses clinking in the kitchen and then water running from the faucet.

"What do we do?" Bunny asked.

"Abort, Abort."

Bunny grabbed my arm. "But I need that bear."

I heard Julia shut off the faucet and then her returning footsteps. "Oh! MoMo, you little devil!"

Julia appeared back in the living room with a glass of water in one hand and a toy in the other. "He found this in Michelle and Lance's room and he insists on playing with it. I hope they don't mind." She set the stuffed animal on the coffee table in front of us and handed Bunny a glass.

It was the miracle of the wayward Winnie-the-Pooh Bear. Bless little MoMo and his grubby, spoiled rotten little hands.

If I were Catholic, I would have genuflected. Surely, somewhere, angels sang.

Bunny gulped some water then coughed a little. She couldn't take her eyes off the bear.

Okay, the eagle had landed. Now we just had to figure out how to snatch the sucker and make a clean getaway. I stared at it for what seemed like an hour, but in a flash of brilliance, blurted out, "My Pooh Bear!"

Yes, I took a risk. The maneuver could have backfired. Julia could have grabbed it away shrieking, "Who do you think you are you stupid, idiot, lying bag of dingo barf? This was a gift from my brother to his beautiful wife in honor of his deep and committed love for her."

Thankfully she didn't say any of that. Instead, she blinked a few times in bewilderment and asked, "What?"

"Well, not my Pooh Bear, but my daughter's. Amber. It's hers." I picked it up.

"But—"

"That's right," Bunny chimed in. "I remember you telling me that Amber left it here the other day."

"Right. I did."

"But I thought you and Michelle were only acquaintances," Julia objected.

"We were – are. But . . . my daughter Amber and her daughter—"

"Son," corrected Bunny.

"Son – Amber and her . . . youngest son . . ."

"Phillip," offered Bunny.

"Right. Amber and Phillip. They're like this." I held up crossed fingers and shoved the Pooh Bear under my arm. "So glad I found this. Thank you. Amber has been so upset. I'll take it to her right now." I was already at the door with Bunny right behind me and poor Julia looking like a robot ready to blow because the situation did not compute. Bunny turned and handed the glass of water to her. "Thank you. I needed that."

I pulled the door open. "Enjoy your visit." Ugh. That was hardly appropriate. I was full of lame comments, but what could I say? *I hope your brother isn't a killer and please don't send the police after me for stealing his Pooh Bear?*

Back in the car, I told Bunny to hang onto the stash until we drove away from the house. We didn't want anyone seeing what we were up to. Julia was still standing at the door, glass of water in hand, when I put my pedal to the metal. There were some tennis courts just around the corner with a tiny parking lot, so I pulled in there.

"Okay," I said turning off the ignition, "let's see the goods." I felt so criminal as Bunny held up the soft, cuddly, and innocent plaything. Poor Winnie. Caught in the middle. Would he really reveal Michelle's attempted assassin?

"'In the Pooh Bear,'" Bunny said. "Those were Michelle's words. This is the one that Lance gave to Michelle when they got married. I'm assuming she meant for me to look inside."

"Do we have to tear it apart?" I didn't want to ruin an item of sentimental value only to discover we were way off base.

Bunny flipped the animal around at different angles, running her finger through the fur. "Look!" She pointed to the seam along Pooh's underside. It had clearly been ripped open and sewn shut again; the new stitching was loose and the thread was a different color. Bunny pulled at the threads but couldn't get them loose. We needed something sharp. I always keep a pair of scissors in my glove compartment, but I wasn't in my own van. I doubted that the grouchy rental delivery man had left a courtesy pair.

"What about nail clippers?" asked Bunny.

"Those I have!" I dug through my purse until I felt the fingernail clipper on my key ring. A mother must always be prepared for nail emergencies.

I started clipping at the threads. "What kind of trouble were they having – Michelle and Lance?"

"How do you know they were having problems?" Bunny asked as she held the bear.

"Your fight in the parking lot. We heard you say they were in marriage counseling."

She got emotional again. "See? I said such awful things that I didn't mean to. They're in counseling, but it's nothing horrible really. He loves her terribly, but she's having . . ." she lowered her voice. "Sexual issues."

"Oh," I said, clipping the last of the threads free. Bunny pulled the broken seam open and stuck a couple of fingers in.

"You feel anything?" I asked.

"Yup . . . there's a piece of paper here . . ." she was working her fingers around and sticking her tongue out as if it might help her get a grip on the paper she couldn't see. My heart started to pump faster. We had just waltzed into a house, heisted a treasured gift, and were about to possibly find evidence inside to implicate a murderer. I was a little scared, but kind of excited too.

"Got it!" Bunny shouted.

I smiled and we high fived. I had to admit, I was really starting to like this woman. I felt pretty guilty for being so hard on her before.

The Cracker Jack prize was a folded piece of paper. Bunny opened it and discovered it was really two printouts that had been folded together. She pulled them apart and held the pages up so we could both see.

The first was a picture of Krystle Jennings. The second was an article from Wikipedia. Reading down, it talked about the "Dynasty Dames" – three girls from Wembsley Women's College in Massachusetts who had robbed three banks in 1982. Dubbed "The Dynasty Dame Robbers" because the disguises they wore when pulling a job were character masks from the famous television series, Dynasty. They had shot and wounded a policeman during their third robbery and had been on the FBI's Most Wanted list ever since. The article gave the names of two, Anita Abernathy and Marilyn Schmutz, but also had a photo of the third, and person of highest interest because she was the cop shooter – KiKi Urbanowski.

"What do you think she's saying – that Krystle Jennings is this KiKi person?" I asked.

"Well," said Bunny, looking closely at the two pictures. "There's a bit of a resemblance."

"That would explain why Krystle disappeared so suddenly. Maybe Michelle found her out."

"Maybe . . ."

"What are you thinking?"

"Or maybe they were partners."

"Why do you say that?"

"Because Michelle went to Wembsley."

Chapter 15

The bear slipped to the floor. Bunny started wringing her hands and mumbling incoherently. I didn't have much patience for her little nervous spells, as they often turned into big Freakoid from the planet Crackpot episodes, but I tried to muster some empathy. "Are you okay?" I rubbed her arm hoping to comfort her.

She reached into her purse and pulled out a bottle of pills. "I just need one of these." She shook the bottle and her eyes nearly glazed over just looking at them. "Maybe I'll take two. They calm my nerves."

"What are they?"

"Anti-anxiety pills. Waldo gave them to me."

"You mean you don't have a prescription from your doctor?" I snatched the bottle from her hands and inspected further. No label. "Bunny, you have no idea what these are."

"Waldo's a psychotherapist. I'm sure he knows what he's doing. He said he gets them wholesale or something."

Things were beginning to make sense. I had never been a huge Bunny Bergen fan, but she never seemed insane. Not until yesterday's episode on my front lawn. "How long have you been taking these?"

"I don't know exactly – a week, maybe. What's today?"

"Tuesday."

"He brought them over last Monday or Tuesday. He's been so kind and helpful. Listening to me go on and on about my problems."

"Have you had any other. . ." I was trying to put it nicely, ". . . bad experiences lately? You know, like yesterday at my house?"

Her eyes brightened. "Yes! I've been having blackouts. Not fainting, but where I don't remember things for a few minutes sometimes. My boys told me the other day that I was walking around the house looking for our dog, Princess, but she died two years ago. I didn't remember it at all."

"You didn't think that was strange?"

"I did. I asked Waldo and he said it was a symptom of my anxiety and I should just double the dose."

"Dose? There's no dosage written here."

"He said take one pill four times a day, or if my anxiety got really bad, two pills each time."

"Bunny, are you crazy?" I shouted. "You don't even know what these are! They could be laced with LSD for all you know."

Bunny's face scrunched up like a dried pumpkin and she started to cry.

I felt like the scum of the earth. Counseling was obviously not my forte.

"I'm sorry," I said. "That was mean and insensitive of me. I'm just worried for you. This is not the way to handle your problems. Who knows what these are? You're probably making things worse by taking them."

She was wiping tears and snot from her face, so I found a couple of mangled tissues in my purse and handed them to her.

"You're right. But I don't have the money right now. My divorce has wiped me out. I'll probably have to sell the house. I can't even afford a car. The Jaguar is my dad's."

"Which divorce? Your most recent?"

She cocked her head and gave me a what-are-you-talking-about kind of look.

"I mean, this isn't your first, right?"

"Yes."

"Oh . . ."

"Why?"

"I'd just heard . . . never mind, it doesn't matter."

"I know," she looked me straight in the eyes. "You heard I've been divorced twice."

"Well, four times actually."

"Four? Why do people say these mean things about me?"

I wanted to melt into the car seat. Surely I had participated in spreading these untruths.

"I'm sorry. It's none of my business."

She felt compelled to tell me her story anyway. "Charlie – my oldest boy – is from a disaster of a relationship, but we were never married. When I found out I was pregnant, the jerk skipped town. Never heard from him again. I married Richard ten years ago. He adopted Charlie, then we had Michael a year later. We bought this house right after he was born. Two years ago, Richard-the-wonderful hooked up with an old girlfriend from high school and slapped me with divorce papers. He's done everything he can to bankrupt me. Now that the divorce is final, he's going back for full custody. He claims I'm not a fit mother. And I can't afford the lawyer's fees. I don't know what to do."

Here I was, a mother who preached to my daughters daily about not gos siping and not listening to gossip. *Don't listen to what others tell you*, I say all of the time. *Find out for yourself.* Geez. With that level of hypocrisy I could run for political office.

"Where are your boys right now?" I asked.

"I took them to Richard's."

"Oh, no."

"I didn't have a choice. I have the gun. I was there when Michelle got shot. Maybe the shooter saw me. I needed to make sure they were safe."

"Okay, well, when this is all over, I'm going to help you with that. Right now, let's get you some chamomile tea instead of these pills, okay? We can go to my house."

Bunny nodded.

"We have enough evidence here to give to the police, so I think that should be our next step. But I want to talk to Howard first."

"I'm really hungry."

"Me, too. I know a guy that makes a mean ziti at Fiorenza's."

"I don't want to eat at a restaurant right now though."

"Me either. Want to order take out?"

She smiled. "Sure."

I smiled too. I liked Bunny Bergen. "Cool."

After failing to reach Howard or Colt, I left a message on Colt's voice mail to check out Oswald Fuchs' credentials as a psychotherapist, and if he happened to run into Howard, tell him to call me. I started the van and motored out of the small parking lot, heading toward Fiorenza's.

"Thank you for being so kind to me, Barb."

"I'm not sure I deserve that, Bunny."

"No, you're a really nice person. Howard is a lucky man."

Since she brought up the subject, I decided to go with it. "Bunny, are you . . . interested in my husband?"

"No! Did someone tell you that?"

"Waldo. He said you were obsessed with Howard. And Colt said you came by his apartment one day."

She shook her head and I could tell she was starting to fume. "It's not what you think."

"What should I think? And why was he called to your house yesterday?"

She turned her attention out the window, watching the scenery instead of looking at me. Finally, she answered. "Apparently – this is what I've been told, because I don't remember it – before I walked to your house, I called the FBI in hysterics." She took a deep breath. "And mentioned his name."

"Why? I don't understand. Why Howard?"

"Oh boy," she squirmed in her seat. "If I tell you . . ." she stopped short of what she was going to say. "No. You don't want me to tell you and you have to know that Howard loves you very much. That's all I'm going to say."

"But—"

"Trust me. You have no idea how much he loves you."

The smile on her face would have comforted me, except I had just noticed a dark car in my rearview mirror that had made all of the same turns we had made.

"Bunny," I said. "Don't freak out, but I think we're being followed."

Chapter 16

I kept my eyes on the rearview mirror as much as possible without crashing the van. When I turned into the parking lot of the Rustic Woods Shopping Center, the car that I thought was tailing us continued on. Bunny and I both breathed a sigh of relief.

We decided we were getting way too paranoid for our own good and had a chuckle before stepping into Fiorenza's. We bypassed the hostess and moved to the Order Takeout counter. Vito Fiorenza, the owner, greeted us with his usual gusto. "Ciao!" he shouted loud enough for the whole restaurant to hear. "What can I get you this evening?" Vito looked Italian but his family had been in America for several generations. His accent was all Northern Virginia.

"Hi Vito," I said. "We'd like two Baked Zitis to go, please."

Vito shook his head. "Baked Ziti isn't on the menu. Can I interest you in some Fettucini Alfredo? Our new chef makes the best in town."

"I know your chef."

He smiled. "You know Frankie?"

"Yup. And I know he makes Baked Ziti – is he here?"

"Sure!" He turned and waved into the kitchen. "I'll get him for you." He whistled. "Hey! Frankie! Someone here to see you! Some pretty ladies say they know you!"

A second later, Frankie appeared wiping his hands on his white but messy apron. He smiled when he saw me and grabbed me for a big hug. "Oh, I'm sorry, I hope you don't mind the hug, eh? It's nice to see a friendly face. I don't know many people around here, y'know?"

I made introductions. "Frankie, this is my friend, Bunny Bergen." Two days earlier I would have pretend gagged when I called her "my friend," but it seemed natural to say it now.

He shook her hand enthusiastically. "Pleased to meetcha." His smile could've lit a city. "Frankie. Frankie Romano. Any friend of Barbara Marr's is a friend of mine."

"We were hoping you could make us some of that wonderful Baked Ziti, but Vito says it's not on the menu."

"No problemo! You want Baked Ziti, you got Baked Ziti. Two comin' up?"

Bunny smiled. "Yes, two please."

"Vito, this is on me – don't charge these nice ladies. I'll cover it." Frankie put a hand on my shoulder. "It's gonna be fifteen minutes maybe. You can wait?"

"Thanks. We'll be right over there." I pointed to the comfy couch in the corner.

We sat down and made some idle wasn't-that-nice comments. After an awkward pause, I realized I didn't have a whole lot to say to Bunny. She evidently wasn't willing to say anything more about her relationship – or lack thereof – with Howard. And I certainly didn't want to harp on the issue with the pills Waldo had given her. So the air filled with the pressing silence that people dread when they don't know what to say next. I scanned the restaurant trying to think of something interesting to say.

Luckily, Bunny finally filled the void. "I love your website," she said quietly.

I admit, I was a little surprised. My ChickAtTheFlix.com website felt more like a work in progress than a real internet presence. I had started working on it before Halloween and the Mafia-in-my-backwoods fiasco that had introduced me to Frankie, but the whole thing still needed a lot of polishing. I hadn't quite figured out how to attract readers other than my family and old Mr. Ebersbacher on Cabbage Tree Place, who spent seven of his eight waking hours on the computer.

"Thank you." I smiled, embarrassed. "You read it?"

She nodded. "I'm a subscriber. I get all of your new articles."

"I'm still working some bugs out. And trying to figure out how to get a bigger audience."

"I love movies, too. My favorite article was the one on *Speed*. That's such a fun movie and what you wrote was really funny."

I nodded. That post wasn't too long ago. "*Speed* - When Keanu Reeves Could Act," was one of my favorites as well.

"I've seen that movie . . . probably at least twenty times," she laughed.

"Seriously?" I was surprised. She didn't seem like an action movie kind of gal to me.

"I love the end."

"When they make out after narrowly escaping a crushing death in the subway train car?"

She smiled. "I know that it's cheesy and not very believable, but I still love it."

I shrugged. "There's too much emphasis on believability. Who needs reality? I love action movies – that's one of my favorites. It introduced us to Sandra Bullock, right?"

Thinking of Sandra Bullock reminded me of Roz, who thinks Sandra Bullock walks on water. She's only seen one movie her whole life, *While You Were Sleeping*, which she still calls *When You Were in the Hospital.* But she loved it so much that she just raves about it and Sandra Bullock. Even though she knows nothing about The Academy of Motion Pictures, she will tell anyone she meets that Sandra should have won an Academy Oscar Award for that AMAZING movie, *When You Were in the Hospital.* I pulled out my cell phone and hit her speed dial number. I had told her I would call when I had information, and I didn't want her to worry.

Roz's husband, Peter, answered and said she wasn't home. The school crossing guard had called her to discuss a school-related issue, so Roz went to meet her. That sort of occurrence wasn't uncommon. Because she was the

PTA president, she got roped into all sorts of things that I considered silly, but Roz took it well and was always willing to help.

I decided to call Peggy and clue her in on what Lance's sister had told us. That's when I began to get worried. Simon, Peggy's husband, said that Roz had called and asked Peggy to join her at the gym.

"That's strange," I said when I clicked my phone off.

"What?"

"Peter said Roz went to meet Shashi, but Peggy got a call from Roz to meet her at the gym. How can Roz be in two places at once?"

I was still pondering the issue when my phone buzzed. Caller ID said it was Peggy. Nice timing, I thought. Pushing the talk button, I started in. "Hey there lady, are you with Roz?"

The response was not one I expected. "IF YOU WANT TO SEE YOUR FRIENDS ALIVE, BRING BUNNY BERGEN TO THE WINSLOW BUILDING ON MIMOSA PARKWAY. WE SENT AN ESCORT."

I think I stopped breathing. I could feel the blood drain from my hands and face. The voice was mechanical and unrecognizable – as if the speaker was talking through a vocal masking device.

The line went dead. "Hello?" I yelled, panic surging. I stared at the phone, not knowing what to do next.

"What's wrong?" Bunny asked.

How do you tell a woman who's already on the verge of a nervous breakdown that someone wants her bad enough to kidnap two innocent women?

The little bell on the door announced another customer who told the hostess in an Indian accent that her friends were already here. A moment later, Shashi Kapoor slid onto the sofa next to Bunny. Shashi had lost her usual Sari, and instead, sported blue jeans and a Redskins sweatshirt. A plain brown baseball cap topped off the unusually American ensemble.

"Hello, ladies," she murmured. She'd also instantly traded the Indian accent for a Georgia Peach Southern twang. OMG as the kids say. I certainly didn't see that one coming. How had my kind, caring crossing guard been roped into this crime? And while I struggled to understand what was happening, I noticed her right hand stuffed suspiciously in her sweatshirt pocket.

Bunny started breathing hard and looked back and forth between me and Georgia Peach Shashi.

"You can tell Bunny what's wrong when we get to your car," Shashi said softly.

"You're the escort?"

Shashi nodded. "Don't be obvious, just leave and if anyone asks, say you'll be right back."

"Barb, what's happening?"

"Bunny, whatever you do, don't lose it. This is no time to showcase your talent for shrill, animals-of-the-Amazon mating calls. Just follow me – quietly. And whatever she says, do it."

As the three of us stood to leave, Frankie arrived with our food nicely wrapped in a Fiorenza's bag. "I threw in some bread and salads for you too," he said.

Grabbing the bag, I suddenly felt very lucky to have befriended an ex-gangster. But I needed a code and I needed it quick-like. The problem was, my stomach churned from fear, and Uncle Ralph was knocking on my esophagus.

"Thanks, Frankie," I said, hoping my grim, green face alone might throw him a hint. "You're a great friend. I'm so glad I met you. Remember the night we met? Boy, that was a night, huh?"

Shashi cleared her throat loudly which I took to mean, move your butt or I'll shoot it off.

"Okay, gotta go." So far my code seemed totally pathetic and entirely undecipherable. That's when I was inspired to spell out the word HELP. "We'll go HOME now," I said. "And we'll EAT these LITTLE ziti and . . ."

Damn! I didn't have a word for P. Potato? Pigtails? Pendulum? Then I had it. ". . . and POP open a bottle of wine."

We were walking through the door with Shashi practically pushing us when I threw one more clue out for good measure. "May the Karma be with you, Frankie!"

Shashi followed us to my rental van. She made sure we were both in, then took the back seat behind Bunny. "Pop a bottle of wine?" she drawled. "Do you think I was born yesterday?"

"Evidently not born yesterday or in India," I quipped.

"You know where to go – get moving. If we're not walking through the doors in ten minutes, they drop one. Five minutes later they drop the other."

"Drop?"

"Kill," I said as I slipped the key into the ignition and turned over the engine. "They'll kill Peggy and Roz if we don't show up on time."

"Who's they?" asked Bunny.

I pulled out of the parking space, around the service road and onto Rustic Woods Parkway. "Good question. I'm assuming you are . . . Bunny, who were those other two?"

"Other two what?"

"Dynasty Dames. There was that KiKi person and . . ."

Shashi seemed stymied. "So you really were on to us?"

Bunny picked up the paper we found in the Pooh Bear. "Marilyn Schmutz and Anita Abernathy." She turned around so she was looking at Shashi. "You're one of them?"

I hung a left. "What do you mean we really were on to you?"

"Krystle said Michelle told Bunny. Did she tell you too?"

Bunny narrowed her eyes at Shashi. "Michelle didn't tell me anything. What would she have told me?"

I stopped at a red light and had a mini-meltdown. "There are way too many questions being asked and not enough answers. First, I want to know your real name."

"I don't think you're really in the position to be demanding answers, do you?"

"See. Another question. What's your real name?"

"Fine – Marilyn Schmutz. Now you answer one for me."

"Deal. But then I get another answer after."

"When did you find out about us?"

I looked at my watch. "About forty five minutes ago."

"What?"

"Nope, now you owe me one. Is Michelle the third Dame?"

"No."

"That's a relief," Bunny said as she fidgeted in her seat. "Oh my gosh, this is such a long light!"

"I know," Shashi agreed. "Don't you hate it?"

"I sat at this light for ten minutes once," Bunny said. "I kid you not."

"The one at Fairfax Park and Poplar Road is even worse."

I was beginning to lose it. Roz and Peggy didn't deserve to die because Shashi and Bunny had traffic light issues. "Can we get back to the information session please? Time is running out."

Finally, the light turned green and I hit the gas. From our present location and without traffic, we could get to The Winslow Building on Mimosa in about four minutes.

"Listen, Shashi – can I still call you Shashi? Because, well, you still look like a Shashi. The southern accent is throwing me."

"Yeah, try growing up a Jewish Hindu in the heart of Baptist country. It wasn't fun."

"So you moved to Massachusetts and became a bank robber?"

"Krystle was very . . . persuasive. She had a way of talking me into anything."

"KiKi Urbanowski you mean?"

"That was then, this is now. She's Krystle through and through. And she's a mean bitch – Michelle found out the hard way."

I was just making a right-hand turn onto Mimosa Parkway when Bunny erupted without warning. She lunged into the back seat shrieking like Bruce Lee on a Red Bull high and in the process, caused me to swerve into the oncoming lane. I screamed at the sight of headlights coming toward us. The car barely missed us.

"Give it to me, give it to me, give it to me!" Bunny hollered while tackling Shashi. I think she had her hands around her throat. It was hard to tell since I was trying to get the car back onto the right side of the road without getting us all killed. Cars honked all around.

I wasn't sure Bunny's tactic was a smart one. "Bunny! Are you trying to get us all killed?"

Shashi was yelling and pulling at Bunny's hair. "Stop it! What are you doing?"

"Where is it?" Bunny's voice had climbed several octaves.

I turned my head briefly to glimpse her rooting around in Shashi's sweatshirt pocket.

"Where is it?" Bunny yelled again.

"What?" Shashi screamed back.

"The gun, dammit! Give it to me."

Shashi pulled her right hand out of her pocket and held both up in the air. "I don't have one."

"You kidnapped us without a gun? What kind of criminal are you?" I looked at the clock on my dash. We had exactly five minutes before they started in on Peggy and Roz and we were only about twenty seconds from the Winslow building.

Making a hard right turn, I screeched into the empty parking lot of the Rustic Woods Golf Course, threw the gear shift into park, and turned around to face Shashi. "Behind that seat is the gun used on Michelle Alexander," I said. "You've got one minute to tell us everything or I use it on you. Start talking."

Chapter 17

I highly doubt that my threat scared Shashi, but she talked anyway. It turned out she did have a gun, but it was in her backpack and it wasn't loaded. Guns scared her, she said. Go figure. At my request, Bunny settled down and climbed back into the front seat.

In fifty-nine seconds, Shashi hit the highlights. Krystle (KiKi) followed her to Rustic Woods five years ago, much to Shashi's dismay. Shashi had a nice, private set-up; she'd made friends, she'd left her old life behind, and she felt secure that she'd never be caught. She figured if she could be successful wheedling her way into that school crossing job without raising any red flags, she was in the clear. She got a little worried when she found out that my husband was an FBI agent, but her real problem was Krystle, who was a class A bitch, control freak, and paranoid lunatic. Krystle suspected that Michelle was on to her after a recent yearbook committee meeting held at Krystle's house. Krystle had stupidly mentioned dating someone at college and that someone had also, coincidentally, dated Michelle after Krystle killed a cop and went on the lam. Krystle was afraid that Michelle had confided her suspicions to Bunny, since they were so close. Certain that Michelle was going to rat her out she disappeared from the scene, but masterminded a plot to have Waldo drug Bunny, stir up some crazy moments, plant the idea in her head that Michelle was talking about her behind her back, then frame Bunny for Michelle's murder, only Krystle didn't make sure that Michelle was dead and no one was biting on the Bunny story. Krystle and Waldo didn't even include Shashi in the details of their grand scheme until after the botched murder attempt. At that point, they decided she was needed for their next ploy.

See, this is what I mean about my life – most mothers use their vans to chauffeur kids from baseball games to pizza birthday parties. Me, I'm stuck in a dark and vacant parking lot with a religiously and ethnically confused, fire-arm phobic fugitive explaining her distrust of a fellow desperado. Where's the justice?

While I would have loved to hear what Krystle's next ploy was or why Waldo was involved, the sands were running thin in the hourglass and if we didn't move, Roz and Peggy were going to the big Mothers Day sale in the sky.

I was about to throw the van into reverse and peel out, when something hit us from behind. Despite the dark of night, the vehicle that had rear-ended me shone in my rearview mirror like a lovely beacon – Frankie's yellow Volkswagen van. He was out and running to my aid. When I powered down the window, I saw he had a gun in his hand.

"You okay, Barb?" he sputtered, out of breath.

"That's not an easy question to answer, but you can put the gun down."

"Did I read your code right? You need help?"

"You mean it worked?"

My cell phone rang. Bunny picked it up and looked. "This says it's Peggy."

I looked at my watch. "Oh man, time is running out." I turned to Shashi. "They're serious about this, aren't they?"

She nodded. "I told you – she's determined."

I answered the phone. The voice on the other end wasn't happy. "Put her on."

"Who?"

"Shashi, you idiot!"

I handed the phone to Shashi and whispered in Frankie's ear. "Get in – this is your chance to make amends."

He whispered back. "Let me move my van. Don't need a ticket for improper parking." While did his thing, Shashi closed my phone. "She says three minutes or they're both dead."

"You know, if you'd told me back at Fiorenza's that you didn't have a gun, it would have saved us all a lot of pain. We could have called the FBI and had this handled."

"Don't worry. That's part of their plan."

Her comment caught my attention but Frankie had returned and was jumping in the back seat next to her. We didn't have time to waste. I pulled into reverse then peeled forward onto Mimosa Parkway. Twenty seconds and we'd be in the parking lot of the Winslow building. That was twenty seconds to devise a plan of attack.

"Frankie," I said, "Meet Shashi Kapoor, aka Marilyn Schmutz, bank robber and one of FBI's most wanted. Shashi, meet Frankie – ex Mafia thug. You two have several things in common – neither of you likes killing and you've both been wanted by the law."

"Nice to meetcha," Frankie said.

"Likewise," answered Shashi.

Ten seconds.

"Shashi, do you want your freedom?"

"Who wouldn't?"

"Work with me to save Roz and Peggy, and I'll do everything in my power to see the FBI grants you amnesty. I have an in, you know. It worked for Frankie – right?"

Frankie nodded. "I'm walkin' the high road now. Feels good."

"Everything in your power isn't exactly a guarantee," she responded glumly.

I made a fast left turn into the large, well-lit lot of the Winslow building, and screeched in behind an overgrown azalea bush to give us some cover while I finished explaining my plan.

"Frankie, is that gun loaded?"

He nodded.

"Can I take it with me?"

"Sure. You know how to fire one of deze tings?"

"Not yet. Show me in a minute. Bunny, hand me that paper with KiKi's picture on it."

She did. "Shashi – we're going to play this out as if you brought us in exactly as planned and we came along only because you had a loaded gun pointed at us. Get that gun out of your backpack now. Will they know it's not loaded?"

She shook her head.

"Good. Play it mean. We'll act scared. Can you act scared, Bunny?"

"I am scared."

"Good."

"And I really have to pee. Bad."

"Hold it."

I handed the paper and my cell phone to Frankie. Call the FBI as soon as we're walking. Tell them one of their Most Wanted, KiKi Urbanowski, has Agent Howard Marr's wife and three others held hostage in the Winslow Building and that Marilyn Schmutz is assisting in KiKi's capture.

"Got it. Let me have your keys too."

"Why?"

"I got more ammo in my van. I'll get it just in case."

"Frankie – I don't want you to get in any trouble. The FBI can handle it."

"Just in case. You know how it is – things can happen you don't expect."

He was right. I handed him the keys. "Okay, show me how to use this gun, but make it quick. I think we have less than a minute left."

We piled out of the car and Shashi pulled her handgun from the backpack while Frankie gave me the low down on packing heat.

"This is my Beretta – it's a nine millimeter. It's got some punch. Hopefully you won't have to use it tonight either, but you gotta know how, just in case." He pushed a button on the side and something slid from the handle of the gun. "This here's the magazine." He held it in front of my face for a better look. "I already filled it wit cartridges. Fifteen of 'em. It goes in like dis." He snapped it back up into the butt of the gun and I heard it click in. "You load the first one like dis," he pulled back the top of the gun called the slide – I knew this from my research – then let go and it snapped back into place. "You're ready to take your first shot now, so don't put your finger on the trigger unless you mean business. It's a semi-auto so you won't have to reload if you have to take a second shot, but there's a safety, so when you pull on that trigger, it won't be easy. Just know when you gotta take the shot, then follow through, you got that?"

I nodded, hoping he was right about not having to use it. I tried to convince myself that things would be under control long before I'd have to pull that gun out.

"Stick it in the back of your pants."

"Like in the movies?"

"Yeah. Just like that."

I did what he said. "It won't go off accidentally will it? My rear end is one of my better features."

He smiled. "You always got those funny things to say. Naw. Well, not unless you reach into the back of your pants, and somehow witout realizing it, slip your finger into da trigger and pull. In which case, I'd say you wasn't so smart."

It was my turn to smile. "You can make a funny too, huh?"

"I'll stick to cookin' and leave da stand-up to someone else." He patted me on the shoulders. "Good luck."

My watch said 9:10 p.m. when we started walking toward the entrance of the Winslow Building. Shashi followed closely behind Bunny and me. My legs wobbled nervously. Bunny looked as white as Al Pacino's cocaine-covered coffee table in *Scarface*.

The building stood taller than any in the area and was typical for modern business architecture – sleek and ninety percent smoke gray glass. For lack of anything better to do other than wish I had packed a spare pair of underwear, I counted the floors – fourteen stories. I didn't realize it was that tall. Even though it was unoccupied, all floors were dimly illuminated. Twenty-four hour safety lighting I assumed. Except for the fourteenth floor which was lit up brightly.

It occurred to me once we reached the door that we hadn't considered other possibilities. Frankie would call the FBI once we were in the building, but what if Krystle's plan didn't involve the building at all? What if they were planning to drive up and hijack us to another location? We never got to hear Shashi's description of their plan. Hopefully Frankie would be able to follow and lead our saviors in the right direction. I was about to try one of the two large glass doors at the entrance of the Winslow Building when it opened just slightly, pushed from the inside. My heart started to pound the way it does on a roller coaster just before you take that long plunge down the first fall. You think surely you're going to die and wonder what the hell you were thinking getting on the ride to begin with. I grabbed onto Bunny for support.

Just before the door opened wide enough for me to see inside, Colt appeared from around the corner of the building.

"Hi ya, Curly! Whatcha up to?"

Chapter 18

Not long after his "Whatcha up to?" Colt was grabbed by the collar and jerked into the building. At the same time, my arm was yanked tight behind my back. So tight that another millimeter of movement and it would have snapped. Shashi was playing this thing real. My arm truly hurt. Bunny yelped. I was hoping she hadn't peed her pants.

"Move inside," Shashi said in a low, hoarse voice that didn't exactly resonate with her sweet Southern drawl. Suddenly I wondered if she was a double agent, playing both sides. Had she turned on me? Was her gun really loaded after all? And why the heck was Colt here? My mind was spinning out of control. Of course, who can really think when her arm is about to break and her dearest friend has a gun to his throat?

That's right. Krystle Jennings, in all of her yearbook sabotaging glory, stood just feet before me in the large three story foyer of the Winslow Building holding a scary-big gun to Colt's jugular. To our right was an unmanned security desk. To our left a statue likeness of Bartholomew Winslow, founder of Rustic Woods, towered high on a concrete pedestal. Straight ahead stood a large wall with glass covered-directories and doors on either side of them. A set of three elevators decorated the far left hand wall. No Roz. No Peggy. Had we been set up?

Krystle was a large woman and taller than Colt, so it was no surprise that she overwhelmed him easily. It was well known that she worked with weights at the gym, often bench pressing more than half the male members. She had very manly facial features as well which all of the make up in the world couldn't really seem to overcome. Her obviously dyed, straight blonde hair was cut blunt just above her shoulders and the square angles of the bangs just didn't fit the roundness of her face. She resembled Ernest Borgnine in a wig. Let's put it this way – she was in desperate need of a makeover on the Today Show.

"Who the hell is he?" Shashi hissed. She pushed Bunny and me farther into the building and locked the door behind her. I didn't know if it was Colt's unexpected appearance or that she'd always been playing me like a gullible guitar. Either way, it felt like the game had changed since we stepped into the building, and I feared I was on the winning team. Like Frankie said, things happen you don't expect.

"Don't blame them," Colt said calmly, even with a gun pressed to his throat. "I didn't know about any of this, swear. I was just following her around, because she tends to get in trouble more often than not." He smiled. "Case in point."

Krystle gripped her gun tighter with those big man hands of hers. "We didn't get an answer. Who are you?"

"Just a friend," he answered. "Obviously, a very stupid friend. You can let me go now if you'd like."

"Thanks for the support," I said.

Shashi pointed the gun at me. "Down on the ground." I played along and Bunny followed. We sat on the cold marble floor while I wondered whether Shashi was still on our side or not. She hadn't taken my gun from me, which was a good sign. But then again, taking it from me would let Krystle know that we hadn't come directly to this kidnapping extravaganza.

Krystle grunted. "Get over here and check this guy out." Shashi didn't seem happy over being grunted at or ordered around, but she took three steps toward Colt and felt around his middle, then down each leg.

"You're awfully forward on a first date, aren't you?" Colt. Always cool as a frozen cucumber.

Shashi stepped back and didn't smile. "He's clean."

"I showered before I came. I always do before a good party."

"I don't like you," KiKi said. "You're not funny." She pointed her big gun at his foot and pulled the trigger. The deafening explosion from the shot echoed in the cavernous space. I jumped and screamed. Colt shouted then moaned. Blood spurted onto Shashi's jeans. I felt sick.

"What are you doing?" Shashi was livid. "This was supposed to be no casualties, remember? Threaten but don't injure."

"That was your idea, not mine."

"Krystle," I pleaded. "I'll do whatever you want. Just don't hurt him again."

"Shut up," snapped Krystle. She poised her gun at Colt's head this time, while he'd fallen to his knees, his face contorted in pain. "Or I'll put the next bullet here."

"This is not what I signed up for." Shashi dropped her arm and the gun down to her side. Like two cowboys in a spaghetti western she and Krystle stood motionless, exchanging killer glares. I cringed, fearing Krystle would pop Shashi next and end any hope of us making it out alive.

Meanwhile, Bunny was hyperventilating and – from the sounds she was making – possibly giving birth. She had cowered behind me as we sat splayed on the cold floor tiles. "Bunny," I whispered. "Think of your kids. Don't lose it now."

"It's just that . . . I don't think I can hold it, Barb."

This was my chance to determine Shashi's allegiance. I raised my hand. "Krystle – or KiKi is it? Um, Bunny has to use the facilities, if you know what I mean. Either that, or we'll need a 'SLIPPERY WHEN WET' sign over here."

Krystle shoved Colt forward and pointed to one of the two doors on the wall straight ahead. "You, move that way." Colt moaned with every limp/crawl he took. She looked at Shashi. "Take Bunny to the bathroom then bring her to the conference room. Barb, you come with us or I'll shoot Jerry Seinfeld's other foot."

I raised my hand again. "I have to go too."

She pointed the gun at Colt's good foot. "How bad?"

"I can hold it."

Krystle had pointed Colt toward the door to the right of the directories and I followed obediently. I briefly considered tackling her, but that would have been like Pee Wee Herman trying to take down Lou Ferrigno.

When we reached our destination, she shoved Colt again. "Open the door."

Colt moved painfully toward the knob. "Just wondering – are you into S&M? You seem the type."

"Are you okay?" I whispered to him.

"I'll be fine. I did like that foot though. We'd grown close over the years."

Krystle wasn't in a laughing mood. "You're a regular Bill Cosby, aren't you?"

"Besides the skin, hair and eye color and the fact that I've never touched a cigar – sure. We're practically twins." His hand turned the knob, but he lost balance and fell into the door. His body weight pushed it open and revealed the answer to the question that had been gnawing at me – where were Peggy and Roz?

They were in the conference room.

Eating pizza.

A long, sleek cherry wood table occupied the center of the expansive room. Flat screen TVs hung on the wall at each end while two more doors and three large, framed color photos depicting the nature of Rustic Woods lined the longer back wall. Quite a lavish conference room, fully decked out for absolutely nothing to happen. Except a kidnapping apparently.

Facing us and sitting in two of the numerous cushy black leather chairs surrounding the monstrous table were Peggy, shoving a slice of pizza into her mouth, and Roz who looked about as happy as Jack Nicholson being grilled by Tom Cruise in *A Few Good Men*. She wasn't terrified. She was seething.

Peggy dropped the pizza onto the cardboard box in front of her and wiped her mouth with her hand. "Barb!"

Colt grunted as he moved to a chair. I helped him sit.

Peggy looked confused. "What happened?"

"Krystle shot him in the foot. You didn't hear the shot?"

She blinked. "We did, but Shashi promised us no one would be hurt and this was all just for show." She shook her head. "But I don't think her name is really Shashi. She has—"

"A southern accent. I know. Her name is Marilyn Schmutz. It's a long story. How are you two?"

"We're okay," Peggy answered. "But if you look under the table, you'll see we're limited."

I bent to peek under the table and saw that their feet were bound with duct tape. Roz's hands were also immobilized, resting quietly in her lap. Peggy's were free to grab her pizza up and take another bite, which she did. "Sorry," she said after swallowing. "I get low blood sugar. Have to eat something every hour or I get dizzy and crazy. It's hereditary. My Uncle Declan – my mother's uncle really – had terrible issues, except they didn't know it was low blood sugar and thought he was crazy. Well, truthfully, some family members actually believed he was a werewolf, but that was because of the hair. He was unusually wooly for an Irish man." She sighed and sat back. "I feel better now. But the pizza made me a little thirsty." She looked at Krystle. "Would I be bothering you if I asked for some water?"

Krystle didn't have to think long on that answer. "You've been bothering me since you got here."

I have to admit, I was surprised at Peggy's ease with the situation. "Peggy, can you really eat at time like this?"

"I have to keep my energy up and my wits about me for Roz. You know she doesn't cope well."

Roz, who had been simmering and silent, decided to defend herself. "I cope fine."

"Not last time you didn't."

"Last time they were threatening to kill us and my hand was broken."

"Sprained," Peggy corrected her in a hushed tone.

"Fine. Sprained. But this time it's me that wants to kill." Roz glared her evil Jack Nicholson glare at Krystle so intensely that I expected to her growl, "You fucked with the wrong Marine!" But she didn't, thank goodness, because really between the two of them, Krystle was the one with the body of a Marine, and in a brawl, Krystle would win.

"What's got your pony all up in a tail?" Krystle asked.

Roz's gaze could have frozen Lake Superior. "You know, it was bad enough that you bailed on your volunteering duty for summer swim team, and that you always turned in your PTA expense reports two weeks late. But that little stunt with the yearbook could have hurt the whole school."

"You're sitting hostage in a conference room while I'm shooting Sit-com wannabes in the foot, and you're worried about a stupid yearbook?" Krystle's tone was incredulous. "And, for what it's worth, I did my swim team volunteer time."

"Timing two heats doesn't count. You were supposed to take three shifts and you couldn't even finish one."

Peggy burped then excused herself before joining in on the conversation. "Three shifts? Really. Then add me to your list of bad volunteers. I thought it was just one."

"Me too," Bunny whispered.

I turned around to see that Shashi, gun still in hand, had escorted Bunny to rejoin us. "Sit," Shashi ordered. Bunny obeyed.

So there we were, me standing next to Colt who sat quietly in the chair nearest to the door, Peggy and Roz sitting across from us, Big Mama Krystle with her Big Mama gun standing in front of the door and Bunny and Shashi to the other side of her. Aside from the deadly firearms and Colt's bleeding appendage, it had all the appearances of a business meeting ready to commence. I decided to call the proceedings to order.

"So, do you mind me asking why you've called us here today?"

"You'll find out when the time is right."

I guess the time was right, because that's when our friendly neighborhood psychotherapist, Waldo Fuchs, entered the room from a door behind

Peggy. A backpacked weighed him down. "Man!" he exclaimed. "It's a long haul walking down those fourteen floors!" He took a moment to catch his breath. "But I'm proud to report that all three elevators are rigged," he said clapping his hands. "We're ready for some live action." He locked eyes with me. "Time for your husband to save the day, Mrs. Marr – you did call him, didn't you?"

The light bulb clicked on and suddenly, Shashi's "that's part of their plan" comment was clear. They wanted the FBI involved all along.

Chapter 19

"What do you mean, rigged?" asked Shashi, who was getting more and more agitated with each minute that ticked by.

Waldo looked annoyed. "Mary, we've been over this with you. The elevators are set with charges on the fourteenth floor. The FBI doesn't comply, we blow the charges and the little ladies fall to their little, miserable deaths. In fact, we should get them up there soon." Just then he noticed Colt. "What the hell is he doing here?"

Shashi wasn't changing subjects and her southern drawl was deepening. "It was supposed to be a threat only. No casualties."

"A threat has to be real, sweet cheeks," he answered. "Why is this asshole here and why is he bleeding?"

"He's a friend of hers," Krystle sneered, pointing to me. "Followed her here. Thinks he's a funny guy so I shot him."

"I know who he is," Waldo said. "I asked why he was here."

"You're doing it again," said Shashi, who had started to pace viciously. "You keep making decisions without me, and I'm sick of it. You couldn't manage to frame Bunny for Michelle's murder, much less actually succeed in killing Michelle. You've been bunglers from the get-go. That's why we're on that damned list. How is this going to work any better?" Each time her pacing brought her near Krystle, she'd throw her a glance loaded with loathing.

"You mean you were drugging Bunny to frame her?" I asked. Of course, I knew the answer to that from Shashi's version of The Krystle and Waldo

Show, but I needed more answers and I needed them without giving away how much I knew.

Waldo laughed. He sure was a creepy dude. Even his laugh seemed coated in slime. And those long fingernails made me want to retch. Men just shouldn't have long fingernails. "Nicely executed, don't you think? Bunny has a paranoid personality anyway, so all I had to do was push her over with those little white pills then convince her to confront Michelle about the awful lies she'd been spreading."

Bunny pushed a few blonde strands of hair from her hardened face. She sat in her chair stewing like a pot of spaghetti sauce with the lid on too tight. "I'm not paranoid," she protested under her breath.

"Come on, gorgeous," Waldo said, "let's face it – you think everyone talks behind your back."

"They do," she retorted.

Peggy chimed in. "It's true. They do. Barb, you said just the other day that she could probably feed a hundred hungry kids with what she paid for those boobs."

"What?" Bunny slapped the table and looked like she was going to stand up, but then she did something awkward with her pants and settled back into her chair, fuming. "First off, they're real, and second off, I don't know why you'd think otherwise. They're not huge or anything."

"No, they're not huge," agreed Peggy, "but you have to admit, they're bigger than Barb's, and they're awfully perky for someone who's had two kids." Then she leaned over the table and whispered, "I think she's jealous."

I loved Peggy, but I was fighting back the urge to grab the gun out of my pants and shoot her between the eyes. "Can we please just talk about how we got here?" I turned my attention back to Waldo, who seemed to be delighting in the banter. "Michelle hadn't been spreading any lies, had she? You fabricated the story to stir up Bunny's emotions." I just wanted to confirm the truth for myself.

"And it worked." He was a smug manipulator.

"What did he tell you, Bunny?" I asked "What did he tell you Michelle was saying?"

She mumbled under her breath and I couldn't hear her answer.

Waldo egged her on. "Speak up, Bunny. We can't hear you."

"That I was sleeping with Howard."

"And it wasn't a stretch, since she and Howard had developed quite a relationship, right Bunny? You want to tell Barb why you've been spending so much time with him lately?"

My stomach did a backflip and the landing wasn't pretty. "You've been spending time with Howard?"

Bunny didn't answer but she set a hard gaze on Waldo. The room was quiet. Finally she spoke, but her generally breathy, sweet voice went deep with venomous antipathy. "When I get the chance, I'll make sure you suffer."

Obviously, there was something going on between Howard and Bunny that I needed to know more about, but at the moment, I really wanted to understand Waldo's interest in this scheme. "Here's what I don't get," I said to him. "Why are you involved? What could you possibly have at stake here?"

"Because I'm tired of wearing this." He reached his right hand around to the left side of his face and pulled it off – his face, that is. Actually, he only pulled part of it off.

Roz, Peggy and Bunny gasped in unison as if it were scripted, which would have caused me to giggle if I hadn't been as astounded as they were. I felt like I was watching a bad take from the filming of Mission Impossible XX.

"Crap!" He cursed under his breath. "I hate it when that happens!" He pawed at his face and hair until he'd pulled enough away to reveal a different identity altogether. Sadly, the mug beneath the mask wasn't nearly as pleasant to look at as sexy super agent, Ethan Hunt. Mostly because Waldo, it would seem, was a woman, not a man. That's why his hair had looked so odd to me. It wasn't really his. I mean, hers. And the disguise didn't improve on her looks a whole lot, if you get my drift. Bits of mask remained stuck to her face and dangled oddly causing her to look like some decaying, walking dead character from a Friday night scary movie marathon.

"Holy shit," Colt grunted. "You really are Anita Abernathy. Damn I'm good."

"How did you know?" I asked, almost more stunned at his comment than the revelation itself.

"I had minor suspicions, but wasn't sure until now. I've been tracking his . . . her history since yesterday. I didn't follow you here, Curly. I was following him. Her. Whatever."

Shashi had neglected to mention this little twist when giving us the low-down back in the van. I wondered if that was intentional and was still worried that she wouldn't be on my side if the going got tough. Well, if I was being held hostage for some sort of ransom, I wanted to know what it was. "So what are your demands?"

"I'm tired of this, let's get them moving!" Krystle screamed. I had almost forgotten she was there.

Colt added his two cents. "My guess is they want their names to be erased from the FBI's Most Wanted List."

"But that's ridiculous," I argued. "Shashi's right – if that's what you're looking for, this is a stupid plan," I said, more thinking out loud than anything else. "So they meet your demands and take your names off the list and erase your photos from the databases. So what? They'll just put them back on when you let us go."

"Not when they see the little package we'll leave behind for them," WaldoAnita giggled, picking pieces of plastic from her face. That's why the threat has to be real."

Those little hairs on the back of my neck were springing up again. I didn't like where this might be going.

"What package?" Bunny croaked.

Krystle's lips curled like The Grinch's when he got that wonderful, awful idea. She tipped her head at WaldoAnita. "You want to share?"

"I'm way ahead of you." She threw a large, manila envelope onto the table and it landed with a THWACK that made me jump. "Go ahead," he said to me. "Open it."

With shaky hands, I reached across and pulled the envelope close, not sure I wanted to see the contents.

"Come on," WaldoAnita said. "We don't have all day."

I pulled back the unsecured flap and pulled out what felt like a magazine. My breathing quickened, when a closer inspection told me it wasn't a magazine at all. It was the size and thickness of a magazine, but the cover was of stronger, glossier stock. The words, Tulip Tree Elementary, were emblazoned in bright yellow across a blue tie-dye themed background.

"What is it?" Peggy asked.

"The school yearbook," I said, flipping open the cover, then turning several pages. "This isn't good." I flipped and stared, flipped and stared. This wasn't the bungled yearbook that Roz had described. This one did have pictures of kids other than Krystle's son. Even scarier, were the pictures of Amber and Bethany, Roz's kids, Peggy's kids, Bunny's kids, not to mention many other neighborhood kids, with notes written under each.

Roz shook her head. "That's impossible."

"It's my own mock-up," Krystle laughed. "You can get anything done at copy centers these days. Those notes you see under the pictures of your kids: we've done our research. Birth dates, social security numbers, school bus routes, soccer teams they belong to, their friends, their favorite places to play. I have to give you credit, Anita. You know how to get what you need out of those moms."

WaldoAnita smiled. "Well, thank you. The disguise helped."

Krystle continued. "We know it all. If our names end up on a list again, we'll find those kids and we'll hurt them. Survival of the fittest and all of that."

My stomach churned and I felt sure I would throw up. Bunny started hyperventilating again.

"But you have a son," I screamed. "Could you really do that to a child?"

"It's because of my son that I have to do this. And trust me, I will do anything to get our lives back." Her face turned tomato red and she screamed, "ANYTHING! Do you hear me?"

I heard her loud and clear. So did Roz and Peggy, who both started crying. My heart was breaking for all of us. How were we going to get out of this? Surely, the FBI would be along any minute and a negotiator would deal with these crazies, but would our children's lives be forever in danger? The only way they would ever be safe was if Krystle and Anita were caught, dead or alive.

It was one of those moments in life, where you feel you are at the very bottom of a place that you couldn't possibly be strong enough to pull yourself out of. You're about to give in to fate. Give up. But there's that littlest bit of something – I don't know what it is – hope? Strength? Stupidity? You know you're not going to give up. You're going to fight the fight. The weakness feels overwhelming, but you're going to do it anyway. It was at the very moment that I felt this power surge when Bunny let out a wail and went ballistic. Literally.

Before I could even blink, she was standing and screaming at the top of her lungs. "I don't think so!" At the same time she dug her hands down into the front of her pants, yanked out a tennis ball and waved it around. "I don't think so, I don't think so!"

It was when she pulled a pin out of the tennis ball that I realized it wasn't a tennis ball at all.

Bunny had a hand grenade.

Chapter 20

I couldn't believe my eyes. "Bunny! Where did you get that?"

"Frankie!" she yelled out the door. "We need you!" She shot me a smile. "He was in the bathroom – he gave me this if things got hairy!"

Simultaneously, Shashi was on her knees scooting under the table. What a chicken I thought.

Colt took advantage of the commotion to push me to the floor and tackle Krystle.

As my face hit the carpet, I caught a glimpse of Frankie's fancy leather shoes then heard him warn Anita. "Don't even think about it . . . lady?"

BOOM! My ears rang and my eyes watered. Another shot, BOOM! People were screaming, but I didn't know who. BOOM! A third shot. The acrid smell of gun powder filled my nose. I said a prayer and begged God to let me live through the nightmare so I could see my kids again.

A couple of seconds after the third BOOM! I rolled over to see Colt on top of Krystle. Neither of them was moving.

Shashi yelled, "Run!" and that's when I noticed that Peggy and Roz were up and circumnavigating the table toward the door behind me. She must have cut their duct tape binds under the table. Not such a chicken after all, and obviously on our side.

Frankie pulled me up by my elbow and that's when I saw Anita in a heap on the floor and Colt stirring.

"Frankie," I said. "Go with Roz and Peggy. Make sure they're okay."

"You sure?"

"I'm sure."

He took off, guiding Roz and Peggy out the door. Shashi was at my side and we both helped pull Colt off of Krystle. Her eyes were open and she was breathing, but she wasn't moving and she didn't look good. She must have taken a shot to her lower abdomen where a red stain grew larger by the second. The carpet beneath her was soaking up a good amount of blood, as well. "For a minute there I didn't know if it was going to be her or me," he said. "You okay?"

"I'm okay. How about you?"

"Scared as shit. Let's get the hell out of here." I put one of his arms over my shoulder and Shashi took him from the other side. The three of us hobbled toward the exit.

"Let's go, Bunny," I said. "And be careful with that thing please! It makes me nervous."

We'd made it to the grand foyer and heard the dim sound of sirens. Any minute now and we'd be safe and these idiots would be on their way to the mortuary or the slammer, whichever came first. I actually didn't care. I just wanted to be in my house again, surrounded by my family. Halfway to the big glass doors that would lead us to freedom, I turned around to see Bunny, fiddling with the grenade.

"What are you doing?"

"Trying to put the pin back in."

"Good grief," I begged her. "Just hang on to it tight and wait until a trained professional takes it from you. What possessed him to give you a hand grenade anyway?"

"The gun scared me."

"How did he get into the building?"

"I don't know. He just said, 'I have my ways.'"

"That sounds like Frankie."

We had stopped moving while I talked with Bunny, and that probably wasn't a good thing. We were still several yards from the door to the parking lot and suddenly, I had a very bad, bad feeling in the pit of my stomach. That bad feeling materialized into a horrifying sight – Anita was very much alive and leaning in the doorway of the conference room, aiming Krystle's gun directly at Bunny. Bunny never saw her.

Before I could shout a warning, Anita took the shot. She fell over in the process, and the aim wasn't so hot, but she'd managed to clip her in the leg. Down went Bunny.

And the grenade flew into the air.

I felt like I was watching a football pass on slow-mo replay during the Super Bowl, only I didn't want to see how this one ended.

After landing and bouncing a couple of times, it rolled along the floor toward the glass walls in front of us. It wasn't close, but I figured it was probably close enough. We made a last ditch effort to duck behind Mr. Winslow's sculpture.

Colt's warning reverberated in my ears. "Cover your heads!"

Who knows what really happened after that? I think that Colt, Shashi, and I dropped to the ground, but I also remember the blast throwing me through the air, so truthfully, I have to say that it is all just a blur.

I couldn't hear a thing after the explosion. I considered that I might actually be dead. But soon enough, a slight ringing in my ears grew louder until eventually I was also hearing some coughs and movement in the rubble. I had to brush dust from my eyes and ears.

"Colt!" I tried to yell, but it came out like a whisper.

No answer.

I tried again. "Colt!" My voice was still weak, but at least a little louder that time.

I started to cry. This was probably a good thing, because it washed some of the dust from my eyes and allowed me to see more clearly.

Finally I heard him cough. A second later he mumbled, "I'm pinned." I crawled on my stomach following the direction of his voice.

"Where are you?"

"Here."

"Keep talking." I coughed. "I can't see you."

"Can you hear me?"

"Of course I can hear you." A piece of ceiling came loose and fell. I stopped and covered my head. It missed me by two inches. "Damn!" I shook more dust out of my hair.

"You okay?" His voice was close now but I still hadn't spotted him.

"I'm okay. Can you raise your hand?"

His hand appeared just above a pile of rubble that obscured him from my view. I crawled faster until I could collapse beside him. Where were those rescue teams?

The statue had fallen across Colt's leg and nothing I did even budged the thing. Four or five feet behind him, I spotted Shashi face down. Unconscious or dead? I couldn't tell.

Coughing and wearing down physically, I scanned the area for Bunny. I called out. "Bunny!?"

She didn't answer.

"Get out of here, Curly."

"I can't leave you and Bunny."

"You heard the sirens. They'll be here any second. You get out now."

He was probably right, but leaving them seemed wrong. Then I heard scuffling from the far back end of the building past the elevators. Something was very wrong. Frankie had made it out of the building with Roz and Peggy long before the explosion, so I knew it wasn't them.

I reached around the back of my pants for my gun only to find it wasn't there.

"Damn!" Quickly and haphazardly, I patted the ground around me. I knew it was stupid to think I'd find it in the mess, but I tried anyway.

"Curly, get out now,"

"But I think Bunny's in trouble." I took one more swat around feeling for the gun and what do you know? My hand landed on something that felt familiar. I took hold of the hard grip and started to stand.

"What's that?"

"It's a Berretta. Frankie gave it to me."

"You had a gun this whole time?"

"Did it ever look like I had a chance to use it until now?"

His face was tight and I knew he was in pain. He struggled to free his leg. "Don't, Curly."

I knew why he argued with me, but my mind was made up. At the very least, I needed to locate Bunny. If Anita had her as I suspected, I could point the authorities in the right direction when they arrived. "I'm going, Colt."

"You've never fired a gun and that man – woman – is a killer."

"Frankie gave me a one-minute lesson."

"Shit!" His face was beat red. "If you have to use it, be ready for the kick-back. It will throw you off."

Standing wasn't easy. Every muscle in my body felt like it had been through two wars and then some. As I moved toward the back wall in the direction of the scuffling, I yelled. "Bunny?!"

No response. I hobbled to the conference room wall, and plastered my-self against it, afraid to look down the long hallway. Then I heard her. "Barb!"

I peeked around the wall just in time to see a door close. Above the door hung a lit sign with the universal symbol for stairs. The way I guessed it, Anita was hauling Bunny to the fourteenth floor where the elevators were rigged. I'd seen enough action movies to be able to figure that one out. "Colt!" I yelled. "They're in the stairwell. I think they'll go up. When rescue arrives, tell them where we are."

The ringing in my ears grew louder and louder until I realized it wasn't my ears – those were sirens and they were getting closer. Help was moments away. I just had to stall Anita at her game long enough.

My attempt to run was mild at best. It was more a limp-real-fast kind of move, but it got me there and before I knew it I was in the stairwell and could hear Bunny crying. I moved up several stairs as quickly as I could until I saw feet.

"Waldo," I yelled. "Anita. Whatever your name is – it's over. Give up. Krystle is probably dying and if Shashi isn't dead, she's just assisted the FBI. Did you hear those sirens?"

"No! I won't give up. I still have a hostage. Tell them I'll kill her if they don't meet my demands."

I wanted to tell her that her demands were insane. She was insane. But I kept my mouth shut. Lunatics don't take well to being labeled as such and I couldn't risk her taking any retribution out on Bunny.

A man spoke. Calm. Collected. In control. "Tell them yourself, Anita."

I knew that voice. "Howard!" I clamored painfully up a few more stairs until Anita and Bunny were in full view. Anita was pulling Bunny up with one hand while holding a gun to her head with the other. Bunny actually smiled a little when she saw me, bless her little bunny heart. Howard was above them on the next flight of stairs, gun aimed at Anita. I knew he'd never be able to take a shot though. She held Bunny too close.

The question begged to be asked, so I asked it. "How did you get up there?"

"Fire ladder. One of the firemen who helped me said he knew you." Howard's light banter seemed odd for the circumstances, but I played along, assuming it was part of his trained agent strategy.

"Russell Crow?"

"That's the one. Should I be jealous?"

Anita was obviously shaken. Howard's trained agent strategy appeared to be working. Man I wanted to jump his George Clooney look-alike bones when this was all over.

"I don't know. I hope so."

He gave me a cursory once-over. "You look terrible." Then he noticed that I was packing heat and he narrowed his eyes. "Did Colt give you that gun?"

"No. Frankie did. He gave Bunny a grenade too, but don't tell anyone, okay? He's trying to make amends. He's a good guy."

Now he rolled his eyes. "Barb, I thought I told you to leave it alone."

Anita interrupted. "Marr – out of my way or I swear, I'll shoot her."

Bunny's eyes bulged in terror.

Howard backed up several stairs. "We have people who can help you," he said. "Just let Bunny go. Deals can be made."

"Leave it alone?" I hollered. He'd made me mad now. "I tried to leave it alone, but Bunny showed up at our back door with a gun in a suit case," I pointed to Anita. "The one he – I mean she – used to shoot Michelle."

Anita shook her head as she inched up the stairs one at a time. "I didn't shoot her. That was Krystle."

"So much for the FBI doing their job," I said.

"We were doing our job just fine," Howard retorted.

"You didn't know Bunny was there right after Michelle was shot."

"Barb, I'm not at liberty to discuss what we did or didn't know."

"SHUT UP!" Anita's scream shook the stairwell and my ears started to ring again. Howard's strategy backfired.

"Okay," he said calmly. "Just take a breath. Anita, we're here to listen to your terms. This can end well for everyone, do you understand?"

Anita nodded.

"Barb," Howard said. "I want you to back down the stairs slowly. Leave this to me." Without hesitation, I started to do as he said, although I felt a twinge of guilt leaving Bunny.

"You too, Marr." Anita was sweating and her face was peeling. "You leave with her and go tell your Bureau to take me off that list. And now I want ten million dollars and extradition to . . . Switzerland."

Who did she think she was, Roman Polanski?

When Howard didn't react immediately, she erupted. "NOW! Or she's a dead woman."

I was inching backwards slowly, one stair at a time when Bunny spoke. "Don't go, Barb," she said. "Do it."

I stopped. "What?"

I could sense Howard getting very nervous. He moved one step down toward Anita and Bunny. "Barb . . ."

Bunny couldn't move her head, Anita had it gripped so tightly, but her eyes slid toward Howard. "It's okay. She knows what to do." Then her eyes moved back to look at me. "The movie. You know the one."

"What are you talking about?" She had me stumped.

"Do what Keanu would do. Take me out of the equation."

Suddenly it clicked. I knew exactly what Bunny was saying. She'd seen the movie *Speed* at least twenty times and she was reciting lines from the opening scene. Keanu Reeves and Jeff Daniels are playing out a scenario in their heads, what to do if someone has a hostage with a gun to their head and you can't get a good shot. Keanu says, "Shoot the hostage. Take her out of the equation."

"Bunny . . ."

Howard was trying to stay calm, but his voice was rising with a little less control than usual. He took another step down. "Barb . . ."

"Do it, Barb, I'm ready."

Anita was freaking. Bunny closed her eyes and I could see her ready her arms to push herself away. I had no choice. She'd started the ball rolling and if I didn't follow through Anita could very well shoot her just from reflex. I couldn't hesitate even a nano-second, or Bunny was a dead woman. I pulled the gun up fast, pointed it at Bunny's foot, and yanked hard on the trigger.

Blackness engulfed my vision like a tunnel. The shot, which should have been deafening sounded no louder than a champagne cork popping. Simultaneously, the force blew me back into the wall and the impact took my breath away. Colt told me to watch out for the kick back but I never expected that kind of power.

All I could see was a pin prick of light and all I could hear was the beating of my own heart. It felt like I was submerged, deep in the ocean, looking up to the surface.

Time seemed to stop.

Then WHOOSH! Like a wave hit me, my vision opened and my hearing returned. The first thing I saw was Bunny, sprawled on the stairs at my feet. She was screaming. I turned my head up to discover Anita still had her gun.

But now it was aimed at Howard's head, as he lay helpless on his back.

If I'd had time, I might have asked what had transpired during my blackout.

I didn't have that kind of time.

And I was thanking the heavens that Frankie's Beretta was semi-auto, because that trigger went much easier the second time I pulled it.

Chapter 21

Thankfully, I didn't kill WaldoAnita. For a few moments I thought I had, and while I was thrilled to have saved Howard and Bunny, killing someone would have been just too much to bear. The bullet did some major damage though, so she was carried up to the roof on a stretcher and flown to the County Hospital in a medevac.

They didn't waste any time transporting the rest of us to the closer, more comfortable hallways of Rustic Woods Hospital. After the first shot, when my vision tunneled, I didn't get to see Bunny pushing away from Anita who then lost control of the gun in her right hand. Anita, being quicker than we gave her credit for, had grabbed Howard by the ankle with her left hand, pulled him off balance then managed to regain her own footing and handgun at the same time. I was probably seconds away from becoming the Widow Marr.

I wasn't hurt, but rode with Howard in the ambulance. He had a nasty gash on the back of his head from the fall. "I love you, I love you, I love you, I love you," I said, planting kisses on his lips, cheeks, nose, and forehead. If it was kissable, I kissed it.

"Gee," he said with a weak smile, "I think you love me."

"Say it back."

"It back."

I swatted him playfully. "That blow to your head didn't harm the bad joke region of your brain, did it? Come on. Say it."

"I love you."

"That's better." I held his hand and we were quiet for the rest of the ride.

In the ER, a nurse who had been on duty the previous evening recognized me.

"Weren't you here last night?" She peered at me over a pair of half-eye glasses.

"Was it only last night? Feels like a year ago."

She looked me up and down. "What angry tornado swallowed you up and spit you back out again?"

It was the first time I actually surveyed my own body since the explosion. Cuts and bruises dotted my arms and I didn't even want to see what my face and hair looked like.

"No tornado," I said, "just a wayward hand grenade. Those suckers pack a punch, I'll tell you."

She didn't smile but she did blink once or twice before shaking her head and pulling me over to a chair. "Sit. Let's clean you up a little." She disappeared, and a few minutes later a small, shy nurse's assistant came by with cotton balls, anti-bacterial wash, and band-aids. Sadly, she didn't have a brush or a magic wand to help with the hair, but at least I was less likely to die of a staph infection.

After the nurse left me looking like a walking ad for Johnson and Johnson, I stood up to see where they had taken everyone.

Someone called from behind the curtain next to me. "Barb?"

I peeked around to find Bunny on a bed, smiling. "Hi!" She even gave a little wave. How Bunny of her. She had already been seen by a surgeon and would be wheeled in as soon as the room was ready.

"I'm so sorry." I tried to be strong, but that didn't go so well. I cried.

This time she was the one handing out tissues. "It's okay. It was my idea, remember?"

I nodded, not convinced.

"The surgeon says you were a terrible shot. The bullet just grazed my foot. I broke my ankle and tore a ligament in the fall."

"You were so brave. I don't think I would have done what you did." It was the truth. Bunny Bergen was my new heroine. I'd never say a bad word about her again and I'd make up for all of the times I had in the past.

"We were both brave."

"And I'm sorry I talked about you behind your back and said those things about your boobs."

"Hey, as I see it, that's a compliment, right?" She smiled then closed her eyes. The nurse said they'd given her an oral sedative to prepare her for surgery and that I should leave her be. So I touched her arm and said a prayer, then went looking for my two favorite men, Howard and Colt.

Wouldn't you know they were right next to each other in the trauma room and no one had pulled a curtain to give them privacy. Roomies again. Neither seemed to mind, although I found it a little awkward. Howard's gash had already been stitched and he was waiting to see if they were going to keep him overnight for observation.

Colt's leg faired beautifully – it was swollen and bruised but not broken. His foot was another issue, however. He was waiting for an orthopedic surgeon to survey the damage and give his opinion.

I sat between them ready to chat for a few minutes before heading out to my mother's. It was too late to take the girls back home, but I just wanted to see them, even if they were asleep.

"So," I said to Howard. "Bunny tells me that she knows you love me very much, but she won't tell me how she knows this. You wanna fess up, fella?"

"Yeah, How ol' boy," Colt said, wincing as he moved a bit in his bed. "Do tell."

Howard looked at me warily. "Did she tell you anything?"

I shook my head. "But with this relationship you two seem to have, not to mention the woman at Fiorenza's . . . well, as Ricky Ricardo says, 'You got some 'splainin' to do.'"

"Do we have to do this here?"

"I'm cramping your style," Colt said. "Nurse!" he yelled. "Can someone move me out of here so these two lovebirds can do their thing in private?"

Just then a very young and attractive female doctor threw back the curtain. "Who's making all of the noise here and where is Howard Marr?"

"I'm Howard - the one making all of the noise," said Colt.

Howard rolled his eyes. I could see Colt was getting to him.

I slapped Colt's hand. "Act your age or they'll send in a pediatrician instead of an orthopedist. This handsome, mature man is my husband, Howard Marr."

The doctor smiled at Colt, but moved very professionally to Howard and started doing her whole doctor routine. She asked a few questions, checked his reflexes and looked in his eyes. She scribbled on her clipboard then said, "I'm admitting you for the night. I want you here for observation, Mr. Marr."

I sighed, sad that I wouldn't have him home for the night. I was looking forward to taking care of him. "Do you want me to stay until they get you in your room?"

He just shook his head and closed his eyes. I thought of pressing him to talk a little more, but wondered if he just didn't feel well. So I kissed his forehead and went to leave.

Colt, still playful, couldn't let me leave without a tease. "Don't I get a kiss too?" I laughed and was about to respond when Howard cut me off.

"Don't you two ever stop? Do you see that I'm here?"

Uh oh. Amber's words came flooding back. "I think Daddy only pretends to like Colt," and "Maybe 'cuz you hug Colt a lot."

"Howard—"

"Barb, would you just go please."

"But—"

He closed his eyes and shut me out. Two attendants came and wheeled Colt to a different trauma room where the surgeon would look at his foot. I couldn't even look at him when they did. I could only think that maybe it had been me the whole time. Me that had hurt my marriage. I cried in the cab all the way to my mother's. Did I want to see my mother? No. But I really wanted to see the girls, so I had no alternative. It was late – 1:30 in the morning – but she had waited up and opened the door after my first light knock.

"Mom," I said before she could open her mouth. "It's been a LONG day and a lot of awful, awful things have happened to me and to people I love. I'll tell you another time but I DO NOT want to talk right now. I just want to see the girls. Promise me you won't ask any questions?"

She stared me down in that way that makes me feel like I'm a three year old caught dipping a finger into the freshly frosted cake. I was gearing up for a fight, but her face softened and she nodded her agreement.

She had put Amber on her couch in the den and Bethany and Callie in the two single beds in her second bedroom. I visited each, kissed their foreheads and felt their warm breaths on my face. It was the medicine I needed. Knowing they were safe, feeling their energy near me. Those are the moments I treasure in all of life – the moments when the love for my children fills me completely. I can't imagine there is any greater power in the entire world – or the entire universe even – than the power of that love.

So when I found my mother in the kitchen putting Oreos on a plate next to a cold glass of milk, I realized that she knew it, too. She sat quietly with me while I dipped Oreos into the milk and cried in between yummy bites. When I was done, she suggested I stay rather than go home. It would be good for the girls to see me when they woke up.

"Where will I sleep?"

"In my bed – you did it all the time when you were a little girl." Of course, that seemed so long ago, but it was true. When my dad went on business trips, she and I would climb into their big king sized bed and curl up together. She had a way of making me feel safe. Sometimes, when my mother's antics irritated me, I forgot how much I loved her.

"Okay," I said, "but no spooning."

"Barbara – don't be a silly goose."

Chapter 22

Somehow we all made it through the rest of the week. Roz and Peggy, it turned out, had been escorted home by FBI agents after a not-so-brief debriefing. Peggy was enjoying the limelight and had exciting tales to tell of their abduction by master of disguise Waldo Fuchs/Anita Abernathy, Shashi the crossing guard, aka Marilyn Schmutz the bank robber, and Krystle Jennings the yearbook killer, aka KiKi Urbanowski the cop shooter. Roz, on the other hand found no joy or excitement in any of it and vowed to move from Northern Virginia altogether. She'd had enough of Mafia and FBI's Most Wanted living in her backyard. Peter wasn't convinced, but Roz didn't care. She told him to march right into his office and demand a transfer – out of the country if he had to. I was sad. Roz was my best friend, so I just hoped and prayed that she would settle down once Rustic Woods stopped buzzing over the whole affair.

"It's like one of those towns in those ridiculous mystery books – murders every week and the same person has to solve all of the crimes," she ranted once after three glasses of wine. "We've become characters in a silly mystery book."

Peggy laughed. "I know, isn't it great? I've taken detailed notes of everything that happened so I can use it for my writing class."

Roz frowned. I'm pretty sure that's one book she wouldn't be reading.

Frankie was pleased that he had finally made amends in a big way, especially to Roz. And Karma rewarded him nicely. In the form of thirty-thousand dollars – the reward money that the FBI offered for the tip that led to the apprehension of the long-disappeared, but not forgotten Dynasty

Dames bank robbers from Wembsley Women's College. He didn't feel right taking it though, and instead, gave the entire sum to the Alexander family to help defray doctor and hospital fees.

As for Michelle, she came out of her coma and was eventually moved out of the ICU. It turned out Lance was never a suspect in her murder, at all. The story had been fabricated in hopes the real shooter would come out of the woodwork and make a mistake. The police had been assisting the FBI who figured Michelle must have been the anonymous caller a week earlier, tipping them to Krystle Jennings' true identity. And of course, who had been working the case? Howard. If he'd only told me, I could have saved us all a lot of time and pain.

When Howard was released the next day from the hospital, I told him in no uncertain terms that I wanted him to come back home. It was time to fix our marriage. I needed him and the girls needed him.

His answer was lukewarm at best. "I'll think about it."

"What does that mean?" I asked, as I drove him to his condo.

"It means . . . I will think about the idea of moving back home." He looked out the window. "KiKi Urbanowski and Marilyn Schmutz are both alive, did you hear?"

"There's a way to change the subject." I actually had been curious though. "You know Marilyn helped us. Things could have ended badly if she hadn't."

"Can't make guarantees. No deal was made."

"She's a good person, Howard."

"It's out of my hands, Barb."

"I did this, didn't I?"

"What are you talking about?"

"Our marriage. It's my friendship with Colt, isn't it? I'll end it. I'll tell him to cool things. Stay away. No more learning to shoot a gun. No more tutoring in private investigation. I promise."

He smiled. "You would do that?"

"Absolutely."

He tipped his head slightly. "Good. I like that."

"And I won't ask you about that other woman anymore, but you have to promise to stop seeing her."

"Okay." He nodded. "I can do that."

His answer didn't sit well with me. Not because he promised not to see her again, but because it was the first time he didn't deny anything. So he had been seeing her. I took a deep breath and wondered how I would get around it in my mind.

"Okay," I said as I pulled into a parking space in front of his place. "Then you'll move back in. I can help you get some things now."

He opened the door and slid out, closed it behind him, then poked his head back in through the open window. "Not right now, thank you."

"But we just—"

"And don't talk with Colt. He's our friend. In a lot of ways, I think he needs us more than we need him. Plus, he pays me rent. I like that."

"Fine, but when are you moving back in?"

"I don't know. I'll let you know."

Damn! For a man, he sure was a hard one to figure out. Suddenly, I felt the need for that Ultra Ultimate Sweet Tangerine Spice Pedicure at La Voila Day Spa. That, and a truckload of chocolate.

Chapter 23

On Sunday morning, just one week and six days after missing our first appointments for pedicures, Roz, Peggy and I pulled up in front of La Voila Day Spa. This time, we had a fourth friend along for the fun – Bunny Bergen. Her foot was still in bandages, so she was only getting a half-pedicure, but she was happy just the same, and I was ecstatic to have her along.

"I didn't know La Voila was open on Sundays," I said as Roz slipped her van into an empty space right in front of the small brick building. Truthfully, the place was practically a ghost town. The entire parking lot void of a single vehicle except ours.

"Nope," Peggy said. "They're open on Sundays."

Peggy insisted we wear pretty dresses and have the whole works done – manicure, pedicure, and makeover. Her treat since she planned to make a ton of money on her unwritten book, *Moms with Guns*. I wasn't going to argue with her plan to pay or the interesting choice of title.

Once we were inside, Mitzi, the owner, closed the curtains, turned on a soothing sounds of nature CD, and told us the spa was ours for the next two hours. There was even champagne.

"Peggy," I asked, sipping from a flute. "Are you sure you can afford this?"

She winked at Roz who winked back. "I'm sure."

It was Heaven on a Sunday. Our feet were soaked and rubbed and scrubbed and dipped in hot wax, then rubbed some more. I nearly fell asleep in the massage chair. Then our hands were given the same treatment. After the makeover, I couldn't believe how beautiful we all looked. I pulled a camera out of my purse. "Mitzi, will you take a picture?" I asked.

"Sure. I can do that."

Bunny chimed in, as Roz helped position her crutches. "Let's do it outside. The sun is shining and the trees are blooming. It will be perfect out there."

Mitzi nodded. "That's a good idea. Here, let me just pull back the curtains."

I was nearest the glass door when she slid the burgundy, room darkening drapes to the side, letting in the light and the view.

"Wow." I stepped closer to the glass door. "Someone set up a party while we were having our own," I quipped. The entire parking lot had been transformed. Three white canopies stood side by side, and the middle was decorated elaborately with flowers, while the other two appeared to protect tables of food and drinks. Women wore spring dresses and men sported jackets and ties. "Maybe it's an after church gathering," I said. I was about to turn around and ask Bunny and Roz if they needed help getting out, when someone in the party crowd caught my eye. I gasped a sort of mini-gasp when I realized it was Fiorenza's Floozy. But my face flamed red poker hot when I glimpsed Howard approaching her. He looked movie star-handsome in a pair of khaki slacks and that new green dress shirt I bought him for Christmas. He always turned heads when he wore green.

While I was still processing the whole Fiorenza's Floozy and Howard at a Sunday church party nightmare, Mitzi opened the door and Peggy literally pushed me out onto the sidewalk then off the curb into the parking lot, closer to the festivities. That was when I noticed that Roz's van was gone from where we'd parked it.

"What?" That was all I could utter. To say I was confused would misrepresent my awareness of the circumstances.

Because I couldn't take my eyes off of Howard or Fiorenza's Floozy, I completely missed Amber running to me and grabbing my hips in a bear hug. "Isn't it just perfection, Mommy?"

I bent down to hug her back and ask her what in the world was happening, when the next thing I knew Floozy had descended upon me all smiles, with her Floozy cleavage practically in my face. Her hand was outstretched. "Barbara, I'm so glad to finally meet you," she said. "I'm Samantha Mills – your wedding planner."

Completely flabbergasted and speechless, I shook her hand. I wondered if I might be drooling, since surely my jaw had dropped a foot. She stepped back quickly and that's when I saw Howard in front of me, down on one knee.

"I'm not very good at things like this," he said. "But here's the thing – I love you. I've never loved anybody but you. And you make my life fun, if not . . . interesting. So I was just wondering if you'd be willing to marry me." He smiled. "Again."

By then, we were completely surrounded by family and friends, none of whom I had noticed before. Colt was there next to Bethany and a particularly smiley Callie was with Brandon. My mother stood next to fire fighter Russell Crow, who had his arm around Bunny. I made a mental note to ask about that later. Peter had joined Roz and Simon had stepped next to Peggy. Even Frankie was there all gussied up in a dapper designer suit. The sun stood above us in a cloudless blue sky and the fragrance of lilac filled the air.

Amber was right. It was perfection.

Since I'd never seen Howard on one knee before in my life, and I figured I might never see it again, I decided to keep him there a few minutes longer and enjoy the show.

"So," I said, "Samantha Mills is a wedding planner, huh? All those late nights, dinners at Fiorenza's – that was your 'WORK'?"

His smile turned into a shit-eating grin. "Honey," he said. "Winning you back is the hardest work I've ever done."

"Get up here you goon," I said, pulling him toward me. We locked lips and smooched for probably way longer than we should have given the audience, but did I care? Not a bit. When I came up for air, I answered him. "Let the cameras roll."

"Good," he said. "Because this wedding was paid for either way."

The girls stood with us as we renewed our vows under the middle canopy, then everyone cheered and the party was underway. Howard and I walked the reception like twenty-year olds in love, holding hands and talking with guests. Bunny sat with Russell Crow. She had her foot up on a chair and the two of them made googly eyes at each other. Apparently, they met when he and an EMT pulled her from the Winslow Building.

"I thought you were seeing someone?" I asked Russ with suspicion.

He shook his head and smiled. "Just said that so you wouldn't be so embarrassed by your mother's attempt to set us up. And now," he winked at Bunny, "it's true."

Bunny practically swooned. In between breathy love glances directed at her studly savior, she explained, finally, what she couldn't before – that after talking with Howard at the grocery store one day, he had asked her advice on how to woo me back. She introduced him to her friend, Samantha Mills, the wedding planner, to concoct a most deliciously romantic wedding to renew our vows. It would have happened earlier had it not been for the Dynasty Dames Debacle.

Samantha had done her job well. With ideas provided by Bunny, she arranged a memorable wedding and reception, complete with a champagne fountain as well as a DJ that played my favorite music from my college days in the '80s. While Howard chatted with some friends from work, I meandered to a quiet corner near the cake, where Colt stood with a cane in one hand and a glass of champagne in the other.

"So, I guess I'm losing my roommate," he said.

"It appears that way. Now you'll have all the privacy you need to be the real ladies man that you are."

"Lucky me." His smile seemed forced at best.

"Are you telling me that you're all talk and no do?"

He laughed. "Oh, I do plenty. I'm actually thinking of looking up Anita Abernathy in prison. She's such a sexy piece of woman. I'm dying to taste her flan."

"How's your foot?"

"Good enough to hobble on this," he held up his cane, "but not quite ready for the dance floor."

"Sorry to hear that."

He winked. "I know you are. Let's face it, with two good feet, I'm a boogey machine."

Howard had wandered our way by then and slipped his arm around my waist. "I guess I'll just have to show her my own moves then."

"Dude," Colt grimaced. "I'm talking about gettin' down and funky to some tunes. You need to get a room for what's on your mind."

We all laughed, and for the first time in nearly two decades, the three of us were comfortable again as friends. It felt good. If there is a happiness scale, I was off the charts.

Oh, and that night, Howard and I did get a room, and he did show me his moves. Over and over and over again. I'm not sure where he learned them, but I'm pretty sure they don't teach that kind of thing at the FBI Academy.

the end.
(or is it?)

Do you want to know what happens in between *Take the Monkeys and Run* and *Citizen Insane*? Get your copy of *The Chronicles of Marr-nia* and read the mystery short, "Missing Impossible," a between-the-novels short story. (available as ebook on Kindle and Nook only)

Karen Cantwell loves to hear from readers. To learn more about her other novels and short stories, and to find her email address, go to www.KarenCantwelll.com.

Made in the USA
Lexington, KY
26 December 2011